A MOUNTAIN OF MISCHIEF

A Clowder Cats Cozy Mystery #3

COURTNEY MCFARLIN

Chapter One

Chaos greeted me as I pushed open the double doors into the lobby of the Valewood Resort. I blinked, trying to get my bearings, as I took in the cluster of loud men standing around the front desk. Typically, when I came to work, the lobby was an oasis of calm. We called it the golden hour. That magical time where our guests were sleepily getting packed up and check-out was still a few hours away.

Wendy shot me a desperate look from behind the desk and as much as I would've loved to slink past, unnoticed, and head to my office, I couldn't do that to her. I pasted on a smile and joined her, opting to leave my stocking hat on. I took her aside as the men raised their voices even more.

"What's going on?"

"They're part of the snowmobiling event that's happening this weekend. They all say they want to check in early, but we don't have enough rooms ready."

Her rounded face was flushed, and she kept darting glances towards the group as I grimaced in understanding. Penny, our head of housekeeping, wasn't a fan of Wendy, and she liked me even less. She ran a tight ship and the odds of getting her to mobilize her team to accommodate early check-ins, particularly from this rowdy bunch, were slim to none. I thought fast.

"Okay, here's what we need to do. I'll try to get these guys set up in the lounge. I'm sure Luke can help me get some refreshments over here to keep them occupied. You call Mr. Marsburg and have him relay the order to Penny. That way, we're not the bad guys."

Wendy smiled and gripped my arm.

"You're a genius. You always keep such a cool head on your shoulders."

I patted her back and turned to face the group, forcing my trepidation down with a big smile.

"Good morning, gentlemen. We're more than happy to accommodate you, but it's going to take a little while to make sure your rooms are ready. If you'll all follow me to the lounge, we'd be happy to supply some complimentary breakfast items and coffee."

The men quieted and the one who appeared to be in charge sized me up. He was a big man, in his mid-50s, and looked like it had been a few days since he'd shaved.

"Well, now, here's a young lady with some sense," he said, casting an unfriendly look at Wendy. "Lead the way and my crew will follow."

I shot my friend an apologetic smile and herded the men towards the lounge. They clomped after me, making even more noise. If the rest of the snowmobilers were like these guys, I was going to need to invest in some earplugs.

"Hey, Edgar! What did you figure out?"

The big man who'd spoken to me craned his head around and snorted.

"Not much, Jim, but we're going with the flow. Never had a problem checking in early here before. If you ask me, it's the fault of all these millennials who think they run the world. No offense, miss."

I gritted my teeth and motioned around to the many overstuffed chairs and sofas arranged around the lounge. A few of the men went to admire the moose head looming over the rock fireplace, leaving me with Edgar and Jim. I ignored his comment and focus on what I could control.

"Great, I'll go see what our kitchen staff can provide. The coffee machines and hot water are right over there on that counter. I'll be back shortly."

I hurried away before they could object and spotted Wendy on the phone as I hustled towards the door. She shot me a thumbs up and I nodded as I headed back outside, pulling my hat down further towards my ears.

Technically, Spring was supposed to start in a few days, but our area hadn't gotten the memo. Fresh snow covered the grounds as I crossed the parking lot, heading for the dining hall. I'd opted to skip breakfast this morning, since I'd stayed snuggled up with my cat Jasper in bed for too long, and was nearly late for work. I noticed lots of trucks and snowmobile trailers hogging space in the lot and walked faster.

The warmth of the hall embraced me as I entered, and the delicious smells made me regret my decision to sleep in. Well, almost.

"Eden! There you are," Charlie Turner, my best friend, called from across the room, waving madly.

That's me, Eden Brooks. When I started working at the resort a few short months ago, I hadn't expected to be surrounded by such wonderful people. It had quickly become a home, and I loved my new job.

I thought briefly about Edgar's group waiting for me to return and decided a few minutes more wouldn't hurt. Charlie was sitting with Danny Cooper, the resort's bellhop, slash valet, slash doorman, and Josh, one of the security team members.

"Good morning, everyone. How was the night shift?"

Charlie was in charge of the front desk at night, and Josh typically worked that shift as well. Danny was on days, but he usually wasn't needed until later in the morning. I suppressed a smile as he jabbed his fork towards Charlie's tray, targeting her breakfast potatoes.

"Hey! Get your own," she said, turning to protect her food, her ponytail flying. "Potato fiend."

"Pot, this is the kettle..." Danny said, giving her a mischievous wink. "Morning, Eden. What's with all the traffic out there this morning?"

"The snowmobilers are arriving," I said, casting a longing look towards the remains of Charlie's breakfast. "They want to check in early and we're completely unprepared. I popped over here to see if the kitchen could help me out with some rolls to keep the guys distracted until Penny's team clears some rooms for them."

"Ugh. Early check-ins suck. I should go help Wendy. I'm sure she's frazzled," Charlie said. "I was heading over there anyway after breakfast to bring you this."

She grabbed a bag from next to her feet and smiled as she handed it over. My stomach growled as I realized she'd packed a few to-go boxes with my favorite breakfast items from the buffet.

"Charlie, you're the best!"

I gave her a one-armed hug as Danny targeted her potatoes again

"Hey!"

"Well, eat them so they'll stop tempting me. It looks like they're already closing down the buffet."

I glanced over my shoulder and spotted Luke clearing trays away. He'd be saving some of the best bits of leftovers for the local clowder of cats like he always did. Most nights, I helped him deliver the food and checked on them, partly because my friend Hannah Murphy had asked me to look after the clowder, and mostly because I loved the cats fiercely.

"I gotta go, thanks Charlie. I'll help Wendy out so you can go back to your cabin and get some sleep. Something tells me we're gonna need all the sleep we can get until this event is over."

Josh nodded and heaved a sigh.

"It's the same every year. These old snowmobilers like to drive fast and drink hard. We always end up breaking up a few fights before it's all said and done. We'll be lucky if they don't kill each other."

I grimaced as my shoulders tightened. I didn't do well with

conflict and in the short time I'd worked here, we'd already experienced two murders.

"Not helping, Josh. See you guys later."

I hurried over to the buffet stand and caught Luke's eye. He blushed, as he always did, and walked over, his gangly arms and legs flying.

"Morning, Eden. Is everything okay with the cats? I'm worried about them with the snowmobilers coming this weekend."

I paused, my request for breakfast rolls completely forgotten.

"What do you mean?"

"That's right, you weren't here last year. I keep forgetting you're still new," Luke said, dipping his head. "You've fit in so well. It's like you've always been here."

My heart warmed as he spoke. Even when I was at home with my family, I'd never felt as though I'd truly belonged. Valewood wasn't perfect, but it was full of great people who'd embraced me and accepted me into their fold.

"Thanks, Luke. That's a big compliment."

His hazel eyes dropped as his cheeks flushed.

"But back to the cats. When the snowmobilers are here, they like to tear through the woods at top speed. I wish there was a way I could warn them. Luna's about to have her kittens and she won't be able to move quickly."

A rock formed in my stomach as I realized how at risk the clowder cats were. Luckily, there was a way to warn them. Luke didn't know about my special ability to communicate with them, and as nice as he was, I wanted to keep it that way. I reached across the buffet and patted his arm.

"We'll figure it out. Maybe we can move them someplace while the group is here, especially Luna."

"You're braver than I am," Luke said, eyes flaring wide. "Have you seen the claws of some of those feral cats? Even if I wasn't allergic, I wouldn't be in too big of a rush to pick one of them up."

"You might be surprised. They're all such sweethearts. Don't worry, Luke. We'll keep them safe. Maybe we can ask the snowmobilers to avoid the stretch of woods where the clowder lives."

He snorted and shook his head.

"It would be easier to move the cats than convince those guys to tone it down."

I winced as I remembered my original errand. Edgar and the guys probably weren't happy that I kept them waiting.

"Does the kitchen have any extra breakfast rolls? A group of them already showed up and they're not happy they can't check in early. I was hoping to appease them with snacks."

He nodded and lifted the trays out of the buffet table.

"Let me check with Iris and I can send you back with a tray, and bring more if they're needed."

"Thanks, Luke! You're a lifesaver."

He bustled into the back kitchen area and I glanced towards the lodge building while I waited, wishing I had time to stop at my cabin to see Jasper before going back. He'd run the clowder for years before I'd brought him to my cabin to help him heal from an illness. He would have some good advice on how to keep the cats safe.

Luke reappeared, carrying a tray laden with snacks that made my stomach rumble again. I looped the bag from Charlie around my wrist before taking the tray, promising myself I'd eat something once I'd gotten Edgar sorted out. Luke rushed around me and held open the door.

A pickup hauling another snowmobile trailer whipped past me as I picked my way through the parking lot and I nearly slipped as I tried to balance the tray. My eyes narrowed, and I ground my teeth together in frustration. This was going to be a long weekend.

Wendy had another group clustered around her at the front desk and she shot me a panicked look as I walked past. Why were they all here so early? From the sounds in the lounge, the men were definitely getting restless, and I picked up the pace.

"There she is. I thought you forgot about us," Edgar said, standing as I approached. "What do you have for us?"

"I've got some breakfast rolls from the kitchen and I'll make sure the coffee machines are all topped off. I'll go back and see what your ETA on check-in will be."

"What's this here?" another man asked, grabbing the bag off my wrist. "It smells delicious."

He tore into the boxes, fending off the grasping hands of his friends while I stood there, silently seething. So much for my breakfast. Before I could even voice a complaint, my food was already being inhaled.

I turned on my heel and marched back to the front desk, already sick of the snowmobilers, and the event hadn't even started yet. I passed the second group and spotted Danny as he wandered in through the double doors.

"Danny! Could you help me with the coffee machines in the lounge? I have a feeling we're going to be working overtime making sure they're full."

"You've got it, Eden. No sweat."

Easy for him to say. I had sweat trickling down my back as more people crowded through the doors behind Danny, talking loudly and whooping it up. I shot a look at Wendy, who resembled a deer in the headlights, as they approached her desk.

It looked like patience was going to be in short supply over the next few days. I tamped down my feelings and hurried behind the front desk to help Wendy. If we all worked together, maybe everything would go smoothly.

Chapter Two

By the time noon rolled around, we were barely hanging on to our collective sanity. Penny's team rushed back and forth, getting the rooms cleaned for our early arrivals, and between the people checking out and in, we hadn't had a moment to breathe.

"Who's responsible for this mess?"

I pivoted slowly as the not-so dulcet tones of Penny echoed behind me. A conversation with the prickly head of housekeeping was the last thing I needed. I forced a smile as I saw Penny in all her tightly starched glory. Her hair, what I could see of it since it was brutally scraped back into a bun, shone under the overhead lights.

"Hi, Penny. I'm sorry for all the hassle this morning."

Wendy let out a hissing breath, and I winced, knowing I'd stuck my foot in it. Why did I apologize? Now she was really going to think it was my fault. Penny was not my biggest fan. Not by a long shot. In fact, she was the only person at the resort who visibly despised me. In all honesty, I couldn't blame her. I'd inadvertently accused her of murdering a guest, but that was water under the bridge, right?

"I should've known you'd be involved. Wendy, what is the meaning of this chaos? I run a tight ship and I did not appreciate

Mr. Marsburg insisting we scramble to get rooms ready ahead of time. It's not dignified."

So much for water under the bridge. Wendy shrugged and pointed in the lounge's direction where Edgar was still holding court. Loudly. His room had been ready for an hour, but his rush to get checked in disappeared as soon as more of his fellow competitors showed up.

"Blame them. I don't know why they showed up so early. They've never done this before in all the time they've come here for this event."

A throat cleared behind us and I turned on my heel again, this time seeing a rather good looking man standing on the other side of the desk. His blond hair peeked out from under a stocking cap and his tanned face held an amiable smile.

"It's the storm. It's supposed to hit later this afternoon and I'm guessing everyone had the same idea of not getting stuck in it. We might enjoy driving our sleds, but not over distances that long. I'm Mark Chesney, by the way. You're new here, aren't you? Hiya, Wendy."

His eyes flicked over to Penny and he gave her a quick nod. I fully expected Penny to explode, but strangely, her skin went a mottled pink and she backed away until she was in the hallway that led into our offices. Interesting.

"I am new, Mark. My name's Eden Brooks. I'm with the marketing team, but since it's so busy this morning, I'm helping here."

Why had I gone into that convoluted explanation? He didn't need to know that. And marketing team? There was just me. Mark smiled, revealing a set of beautiful teeth. His greenish gray eyes twinkled. Wendy let out a tiny gasp and wrung her hands together.

"It's nice to meet you, Eden. Wendy, you look prettier each time I see you. From the noise coming from back there, it sounds like Edgar Hanson's already here. No rush for my room, ladies. I'll just hang around until it's time to check in."

He patted the desk with a powerful hand, dropped a wink in my direction, and headed off towards the lounge. Am I ashamed to say

Wendy and I watched him go? Maybe. Just a little. Wendy fanned herself as she turned back to me, eyes open wide.

"My gosh, he's just so..."

"Ruthless? A libertine playboy?"

We turned to see Penny standing back behind us, her face back to its usual stern lines. Her neck was still flushed, and she was playing with the buttons on her collar, seemingly without noticing. Very interesting.

"He seemed nice," I said. "You've obviously met before?"

She focused back on me, her dark eyes filled with menace, and poked me hard in the chest with one of her pointy nails.

"Mind your own business. Men like that should be put down. I'm going back to work, something you ladies obviously know nothing about. I will inform Mr. Marsburg about this fiasco and your poor handling of it."

I resisted sticking my tongue out at her retreating, but it was a close thing. Once the rapping sound of her heels on the tile faded away, I let out a whistle and turned to Wendy.

"Do I want to know?"

"Probably not, but I do," Wendy said, leaning close so she could whisper. "Do you think they…?"

Images of the tightly laced Penny with the laconic Mark threatened at the edge of my vision and I shook my head quickly to dispel them.

"Ew, no. I definitely don't want to know. You don't think she'll report us, do you? We've been doing our best to help smooth everything over."

Wendy waved a hand and blew a raspberry.

"Even if she did, our boss can tell it's just sour grapes. He's a good guy."

James Marsburg was more than that. He was the best boss I'd ever had, and one of the nicest people I'd ever met. Just weeks ago, he'd been blamed in the death of his ex-fiancee here at the resort, and we'd all worked to clear his name.

"True. I don't know why I worry so much."

Thoughts of the clowder cats filtered into my mind and I

glanced at the clock. If we got a break in the mad rush, I could take my lunch and try to find the cats in the forest to warn them.

A couple approached, their hands full of luggage, and I straightened up, smiling as they neared the desk.

"I'm so sorry we're checking out late. If you need to bill us extra, that's okay," the woman said, ignoring the look of fury the man shot her.

I shook my head and smiled.

"I don't think that will be necessary. I hope you enjoyed your stay with us."

"We did," she said, elbowing the man in the side. "We'll definitely be back."

He gave me a curt nod as he handed over the keys, and they walked out before I could print up their receipt. Danny jogged up, his face flushed as his hair fell down into his eyes. He blew upwards dramatically and leaned against the desk.

"I can't remember the last time I've been run off my feet this much. Please tell me it's slowing down."

I craned my neck around him as my stomach let out an embarrassingly loud rumble.

"I think it's getting better," I said, placing a hand on my midriff to quell my angry tummy.

"You didn't get to eat, did you?" Danny asked, frowning. "Have lunch. I'll help Wendy until you get back."

Danny was many things. A potato thief, an obnoxious joker, and someone who was deeply in love with Charlie, although he was too afraid to admit it. He was also a stand-up friend.

"Are you sure? Wendy, is that okay?"

"Of course," she said, giving me a little push. "You're too skinny as it is. We can't have you wasting away. Thanks for saving me this morning. I couldn't have done it without you."

I grabbed my coat and hat before she could change her mind. I'd have enough time to run to my cabin, make lunch, and talk to Jasper before heading into the forest.

"Thanks, Wendy. Thanks, Danny."

They waved as I jogged out the doors, turning my face up to the sky. Ominous clouds billowed overhead, blocking out the blue sky. Huh. It looked like Mark Chesney was right. A storm was definitely coming. I hurried on, even more determined to get to the cats. I'd need to make sure they were prepared for the storm, too.

I unlocked the door to my cabin and spotted Jasper where he was pacing through the tiny room, ears laid back.

"There you are. I was worried about you. I've heard lots of noise going on out there. What's happening?"

I smiled as I shut the door behind me. I hadn't been able to talk to cats for long, and the novelty hadn't worn off. I didn't think it ever would. I scooped him up into a hug, tickled that somehow I'd been lucky enough to be blessed with this ability.

"It's okay, Jasper. It's the snowmobilers. They're all arriving early to beat the storm."

He let me cuddle him for a few seconds before squirming around. Jasper was a senior cat and wasn't used to human contact. He'd lived as a feral for many years, but from the hints I'd picked up from our late-night conversations, at one time he'd been owned by someone.

"That's right," he said, hopping down onto the floor. "I'd forgotten about that. We'll need to make sure Fig knows."

"I'm on it," I said, moving into the kitchenette portion of the room so I could make a sandwich. "Do you want to come with me?"

"I do," he said, giving me a sharp nod before sharpening his claws on the rug.

I winced, hoping he wouldn't tear it apart too much. I'd bought him a cat tree with a scratching post, but he still preferred taking out his frustrations on the poor rug. Fig, a surly brown cat with a heart of gold, had been Jasper's deputy until he moved in with me. She ran the clowder with a competent paw, but my cat still liked to check on his charges from time to time.

I slapped some peanut butter and jelly on two pieces of bread and cut it into triangles before stuffing one into my mouth. Ah. Now that's the stuff, right there. I wrapped the other triangle in a paper towel and shoved it into my coat pocket. I'd eat it on the way to the forest. Luckily, it wasn't a long walk. I motioned to the insulated bag I'd bought Jasper, and he gave it a mutinous look before climbing in.

"I can walk, you know."

"I know," I said, patiently zipping him in. "But it's freezing today, and there are a bunch of people around, all driving big trucks. I couldn't take it if something happened to you."

He gave a couple of cranky mutters, but he couldn't stop the purr that bubbled deep in his chest as he settled into the plush lining. I looked around my cabin one more time before grabbing an apple and stuffing it into my pocket with the sandwich.

"Let's go!"

I locked my door and headed out, past the other cabins, choosing to take the long way around, instead of going past the dining hall. As much as I appreciated Luke's help with feeding the cats, I needed some alone time with them so we could talk without the threat of being overheard.

"There's a storm coming."

I looked up at the sky again and nodded.

"I haven't paid attention to the weather, but it sure looks like it. I hope we won't get too much snow."

"It never lasts long this time of year, but that's not what I meant. There's a strange scent in the air and it's not from the snow."

I waited for him to continue, but he went quiet. The only sound was my feet crunching through the snowpack. A sense of disquiet crept down my spine, but I shook it off. I already had enough to worry about on my plate. Once I got the clowder taken care of, I'd ask him to go into more detail. I stepped into the tree line and put down his bag, unzipping it so he could roam around.

I'd picked the clearing where Luke and I fed the cats at night, knowing they usually had at least one cat on watch in the area. Fig would hear of our arrival soon enough. I bit into my apple, enjoying the spurt of juice, and chewed. Jasper hopped onto a rock and curled up, content to wait for his friends.

I'd just finished the apple when Fig came strolling into the clearing, her brown fur glistening in the weak rays making their way through the clouds.

"This is unexpected. Hello, Jasper."

"We wanted to warn you about the men coming," Jasper said, hopping down so he could sniff his old deputy. "It's that time of year again."

Fig's lip curled into a snarl and she worked her claws into the snow.

"This complicates things. Luna's kitting and it's not going well. I'm glad you showed up, human. We need help."

My heart dropped quicker than the apple core that fell from my hand, bouncing on the snow. This was terrible news. If the competent Fig was asking for help, things were much worse than they seemed.

Chapter Three

My duties at the resort paled compared to the emergency Luna was facing. Jasper and I followed the grim faced Fig through the trees as she led us to the secret place where the clowder lived. It was becoming harder for me to keep up as the trees thickened. Fig stopped as I struggled to untangle myself from a thorny shrub.

"I forgot you're not as agile as we are," she said, wrapping her tail around her flanks. "But there's a reason we chose this spot."

For once, Fig wasn't tossing in a few choice remarks about humans, which only made me worry more. She wasn't the biggest fan of our species, and given the struggles they faced, I couldn't blame her. I fought free of the shrub and straightened, red faced, as I pulled my hat back down to my ears.

"I'm so clumsy. How much further?"

"Just a few tail lengths and we'll be there. Once we're in the clearing, you'll fit better," Jasper said, giving me a head nod.

We pushed forward, and I made it to the clearing without further incident. Once inside, my mouth fell open as cats came to greet us. I wasn't sure what I expected, but the cats were so organized. It looked like each one had their own den, plus communal spaces in the middle.

"Eden! I wasn't expecting you here," Willow said, her tortoise-shell fur stark against the snowy backdrop. "Any news on Charity or Dex?"

The friendly little cat had recently gone on a mini road trip with Jasper and me, and another cat, Dex, as we searched for the small human he'd been separated from. I hadn't talked to Ethan Rhodes, the local detective who'd helped me remove the little girl from an abusive household recently, but the last I'd heard, Charity was thriving.

"They're both doing well," I said, dropping to one knee as more cats crowded around. "Her grandmother took them both in and it sounds like Charity's growing like a weed."

Willow dipped her head, and I spotted another cat I knew, Ollie, as he crept closer. Ollie was a rotund tuxedo cat who never seemed to lose weight, even though it was winter and the wild game was much scarcer.

He sniffed me thoroughly before settling back on his haunches.

"Hmm. You didn't bring any treats."

His little face looked so disappointed, and my heart sank.

"You get plenty of food, greedy guts," Jasper said, his tone sharp. "I've never known you to go hungry. Eden will bring food later. We're here to warn you about the men coming."

Murmurs went through the clowder and I turned as I heard a cat hiss behind me. For a second, I thought I was seeing double, as I saw another tuxedo cat right behind me, but on second glance, he was much thinner than Ollie, and his little nose was black, not pink. His labored breathing worried me.

"Stop that hissing, Benny. I told you until you're better you can't join us," Fig said, tail lashing as she approached the cat. "I'm sorry, but with the new kits coming, we can't risk them getting sick. None of us can afford an illness with the weather and the coming disruption."

"What do the men want?" Willow asked, her soft voice laced with panic. "They're not cutting down the forest, are they?"

Fig cursed under her breath and stood, her tail high.

"I need to check on Luna. Eden, come with me. Jasper, can you tell everyone what's going on? There are several new members who aren't familiar with this event."

I marveled at her efficiency as I followed her to a low-lying shrub at the corner of the clearing.

"She's in here," Fig said, dropping her voice down. "Let me check on her first. Oscar went out to hunt for her, but he'll be back soon."

I stood and shifted on my feet while I listened to Jasper describe the safety measures the cats needed to follow over the weekend. My heart sank as I realized just how at risk the cats were from the men on sleds who likely didn't know they were disrupting the cat's lives and habitats. After meeting Edgar and his crew, I realized they likely might not even care. Fig's head popped out from the shrub and she blinked at me.

"All the kits are here, but they're small and weak. Luna has agreed to allow you to see them, but keep your great booming voice soft. You'll need to flatten down to see them."

The packed snow around Luna's den was hard, but I didn't mind. This was my first chance to see kittens newly born, and I couldn't believe Fig was allowing this opportunity. I lay flat and pushed my head under the bush, snagging my hat right off my head. A soft laugh came from Luna as my eyes adjusted to the darkness inside the den.

"You look so funny," she said. "All three made it, and they're hungry."

Luna's beautiful white coat was dirty, and even though she sounded happy, I didn't miss the thread of weakness in it. She'd had an ordeal and the thought of her, and these three helpless babies suffering through a snowstorm, made my heart clench.

"Luna, there's a storm coming, and it's the weekend the snow-mobilers come. Would you like to come back to my cabin with me? I can keep all of you safe and warm. At least until the storm passes. I know you mentioned..."

I trailed off, realizing Fig was close enough to hear me. Luna had asked if I would take the girl kitten and find her a human home, but I didn't know if she'd shared that with Fig. Luna's eyes softened and she looked at the tiny forms suckling.

"If Fig thinks it's best, I won't argue. Oscar might have an issue with it, though. I'm just so tired."

Kitting was strenuous work, even in good conditions, and Luna and Oscar had picked the absolute worst time to have a litter. Fig grumbled next to me and I nearly jumped when I felt her cold nose on my arm.

"I'll deal with Oscar. You both knew the risks and did this, anyway. There's no reason the kits should suffer for your folly. You have my blessing, Eden, to help them how you see fit."

Maybe she knew about Luna's wish. My mind raced as I tried to figure out how to transport the mama cat and kittens back to my cabin.

"Do you mind riding in a carrier?" I asked, remembering I'd brought Jasper's bag. "It will be a tight fit, but I can go slowly and make sure you don't get jostled."

Luna nodded, her eyes closing as she put her head down. I exchanged a quick glance with Fig before sliding out from underneath the shrub.

"I'll have to go back for the bag," I said as I straightened. "It will take a few minutes. I appreciate you letting me help."

"If you can go before Oscar returns, it would be best. I'll deal with him. He won't be happy, but it's better than losing Luna and her kits."

I nodded and skirted past the other cats, nearly jumping as Benny hissed and spit at me. Fig heaved a sigh and trotted after me.

"I'll go with you to make sure you don't get lost."

She gave the tuxedo cat a wide berth before loping ahead. I retraced my steps, breathing hard as I squeezed through the trees. Once we were back at the rock, I grabbed the bag and flattened it down to make it easier to fit through the close brush.

"What's wrong with Benny?"

Fig sighed again and batted at the snow with a brown paw.

"He's a new arrival we took in a week ago. He got sick yesterday and I'm trying to keep him separate. The breathing sickness can run through a clowder fast, especially with kits."

I held the bag to my chest and made a quick decision.

"I can take him too, if he'll come. The vet who helped Jasper may be able to help him. He doesn't sound good."

Fig huffed a sharp laugh before giving a little kitty shrug.

"If you can convince him to go with you, he's all yours. He's not the most personable cat, but that could be because he's sick. There's little I can do for him and the last thing I need is a clowder full of sick cats."

We hurried back to their clearing, and I was surprised to see Luna standing at the entrance to her den, flanks heaving. She looked so tiny and desperate as she held one of the kits in her mouth.

I put the bag back to rights and held the door open for her.

"You can curl up there with your kittens. It's a long walk, but I'll try to make sure you're all comfortable."

One by one, she carried the kits out of her den, as the other cats watched. Jasper's eyes shone with love as he blinked at me. I knew our little cabin was about to get more cramped, but it was obvious he didn't mind. He walked over to join us, sniffing Luna before she curled up around her kittens.

Fig nodded before looking at the rest of the cats.

"All right everyone. You know the drill. I want the hunting parties to go out and find everything you can. The game will soon hide once those men come roaring through here. We need as much as we can get our paws on. We'll store it all in our cache. The coming snow will at least be helpful in keeping everything fresh. To work everyone. Benny, you are to go with Eden. No hissing. Be a gentleman. She's going to help you."

She took a tremendous leap into the trees, her brown coat disappearing almost instantly as the rest of the cats scattered, leaving Jasper and me behind with Benny. Jasper stayed put, giving Benny a look that was a little standoffish, but not overly unfriendly.

The tuxedo cat's greenish eyes were wary as I approached. He hissed at me before scrambling off into the trees. I started towards him, but Jasper's voice stopped me.

"He's not ready, Eden. If you chase him now, he'll just run faster and hurt himself trying to get away. That sickness is bad. He still needs help, though. I think he knows it and that's why he's so ornery. Trust me, I've been there. It takes a big cat to admit you need help. You can try again later and hope he agrees then. Fig will sort him out."

My heart sank as I looked into the forest. I hated leaving a sick cat behind. Luna meowed softly in the carrier and I straightened. Right now, taking care of her and the kits had to come first.

"Let's go, guys, and get you into a warm spot."

"They can have my bed, but you'll need to make a space to keep those kits corralled. In a few days, they'll be ready to crawl all over the place."

Responsibilities weighed heavily on my shoulders as I carefully picked up Luna and made my way back to the treeline. Just when I thought this weekend couldn't be any more stressful.

Jasper followed, cavorting through the trees like a cat half his age, tossing snow up as he ran. I couldn't help but share his joy as he skittered ahead. It was good to see him having fun. Somehow, I was going to figure out how to house a mama cat, her three babies, and track down a very sick cat who needed to be quarantined. I didn't know how I was going to manage that, particularly with the madness going on at the resort, but somehow I'd find a way.

Chapter Four

Miraculously, the resort's lobby was silent and there wasn't a single sign of any snowmobilers around. I checked my watch and heaved a sigh of relief when I realized I'd only taken a little over an hour for lunch.

Danny popped his head out of the hallway and smiled when he saw it was just me and not a guest.

"Whew, I thought I was busted when I heard those doors," he said, talking with his mouth crammed full of food.

"That's a lovely visual. Where's Wendy?"

He swallowed hard before shoveling more chips into his mouth.

"It really slowed down, so I had her take her lunch. We've got about two hours before check-in time begins for real."

Okay, so first, I needed to stop asking him questions while he was eating, and second, I needed to figure out just how many more people we'd be dealing with. I hung my coat up and typed on the computer to pull up our booking logs.

Danny hopped onto the desk and peered at the computer, crunching merrily away. He looked down at the bag before looking at me. I couldn't help but chuckle at the look on his face.

"I had lunch and you don't need to share those with me."

"Good thing, cuz there's only like two chips left. Whatcha doing?"

"I'm seeing just how many more people we can expect for the rest of the day. I don't even want to ask Penny how the house-keepers are doing with the rest of the rooms."

"I saw her yelling at Alicia and Jenny a little while ago, so yeah, probably want to avoid her for a while. What's the computer say?"

I looked back at the screen and started tallying up the guests.

"At least another fifteen people. Wow! I don't think I've ever seen this place that full."

"Yeah, this is a pretty big deal. Have you checked the weather? I have a feeling I'll have to help Carl with the shoveling and plowing if it's as bad as they're saying it's going to be."

I opened my browser window and my heart sank when I saw the weather alert highlighted in red.

"Red's the worst color, right?"

Danny hopped down and let out a low whistle before reading the alert.

"Strong winds, two feet of snow, and blizzard like conditions. It's a good thing everyone staying here brought their own snowmobile. That's going to be the only way to get around for the next few days."

I drummed my fingers on the desk before scrolling down a little further.

"When's it supposed to start?"

"We've got a few hours. I suppose if the rest of the people checking in don't make it before this evening, they're going to cancel. Dang it, I needed a few things from town, and I don't think I'll make it there and back in time."

"Whatcha need? The kitchen's all stocked with food and such, so we don't need to worry about that. Although, I sure hope they remembered to order plenty of alcohol. This group can put down some beers."

"I'm helping a cat and her kittens and I want to make sure they have a safe place once the kittens move around. And I don't even know what they're going to need."

"Sweet! One of the feral cats, huh? Can I see them?"

I thought about Luna and didn't know what to say. She was friendly enough with me, but I didn't think she was a huge fan of humans.

"Maybe. They're only a few hours old, though."

"My sister used to raise cats back when I was still in high school. I've got it. One second, I'll be right back."

He disappeared into the hallway and I could hear the faint sounds of him rummaging. I checked the doors before walking back to see what he was doing. The door to the storage room was propped open, and I heard a crash.

"Oops. Here we go. I thought I remembered this being back here. Eden?"

"I'm right here. What do you have?"

He struggled out through the doors, carrying a netted thing folded in half.

"A playpen! It's made for babies, but my sister used to use one for her cats. I don't think the resort will need it for a while. We don't get many babies."

I lit up as I helped him carry it back to the front desk. It was perfect. I could give Luna her freedom and keep her safe, without worrying about kittens being underfoot. It was a lot better than my plan to lock them in my tiny bathroom.

"Thanks, Danny. You're a genius!"

His chest puffed out, but the cheerful look on his face faded quickly as he looked behind me. I turned and winced as I saw Penny standing there, her arms folded across her thin chest.

"And what are the two of you doing that was so important you abandoned your post? Why do you have that playpen out? That's strictly for guest use only."

My mind raced for an explanation, but Danny beat me to it.

"It was a guest request, Penny. I'm surprised housekeeping isn't taking care of it, but don't worry, we've got this."

Her brown eyes narrowed as she looked at us. I focused on keeping a noncommittal look on my face while Danny smiled. She bought it, or at least appeared too.

"We need to have someone up front. You know that, Eden. I expect little from this one here, but I thought you at least had some brains in that head of yours. Maybe you lost them all when you cut your hair, like Samson and his powers."

And with that unfriendly swipe, she marched off, heels ticking loudly on the floor. I bit back several choice comments and let out my breath through my nose, hoping it would calm me.

"Ignore her. She fuels herself with nastiness. Besides, I think your hair looks great. Charlie did an excellent job."

I touched the ends of my hair, still surprised that they stopped by my shoulders instead of my waist.

"Thanks, Danny. And thanks for covering for me. You don't think she'll check on our story?"

"Nah. As soon as Wendy's back, I'll help you take this to your cabin and we can get it set up. Oh! I'll grab some extra towels and such from the laundry. I'll make sure they're the old ones destined for recycling, so don't worry. This will be fun!"

He jogged off again, and I shook my head, marveling at his energy. The elevators dinged, and I hurried back to the computer. I barely recognized Edgar, decked out in his warmest gear, as he walked past with a few of his teammates. He didn't even look my way as they walked past, heading outside.

Wendy came through the door right after they left, rubbing her gloveless hands together.

"Brrr! The temperature is really dropping out there. Did anything exciting happen while I was gone? Where's Danny?"

"He's grabbing something from the laundry. He was here when I got back, though. Did you have a pleasant lunch?"

She unwrapped her scarf and hung her things next to mine on the hooks, nodding.

"It was quiet, and that's just what I needed. It's so nice having our housing here on site. It means we can have solitude whenever things get a little hairy here. How about you?"

"It was nice. At least things have settled down. Any snow out there yet?"

"Not yet, but you can smell it. If you need to catch up on your work, go ahead. I can take over the desk. What's this playpen doing here? Never tell me the snowmobilers brought a baby along with them?"

"Oh, no. It's for me. I took in a cat who just had kittens, and Danny had a great idea to use that to keep them safe."

Wendy's eyes lit up.

"Kittens! Oh, how wonderful. How big are they? What color are their eyes?"

"They were just born, so I don't know for sure. I think all that changes, doesn't it? Honestly, I need to learn more about caring for kittens. There's so much I don't know."

"What colors are the parents? I'm guessing it's one of the wild cats you always take care of? Is she nice?"

"She's a dear. She's white, and the father is a black cat with blue eyes. His name's Oscar."

"How precious! I hope I can come see them."

Once everyone found out about the kittens, they were going to be pretty popular. Everyone would want to see them. Well, except Penny.

"I think I will go back to my office, but if it gets crazy again, just holler and I'll come help."

On my way back to my office, I noticed that Mr. Marsburg's office was closed and dark. Ever since his former fiancee had been murdered at the resort, he'd been spending less and less time there, relying on us to make sure everything was running smoothly.

I flipped my light on and sat behind my desk, exhaling. I'd planned to work on a new marketing campaign for the resort's spring and summer seasons, but all of my inspiration had been chased away by demanding guests. I checked the wall clock and shrugged. I only had another hour before more people were due, and it made little sense to start an extensive project now. Instead, I opened my browser and began learning about caring for kittens.

By the time I was staring in horror at my screen at the myriad of things that could go wrong, I heard Danny behind me.

"Relax, Eden. We've got this. They say it takes a village to raise a child. Well, you've got an entire village here ready to help raise these kittens. I've got the towels, so let's head to your cabin and we'll check on them."

Heartened, I shut my computer down and grabbed for the towels as Danny tossed them to me. They were a little on the ragged side, but they were way softer than the cold, hard surface of Luna's clowder den. I waved to Wendy as Danny grabbed the playpen and headed outside, forgoing my coat for the quick trip.

I followed Danny through the parking lot to take the shortcut back to our cabins and heard a roaring engine flash by. An icy spray of slush drenched me as I turned my back just in time to avoid getting the towels soaked.

Laughter echoed past as the driver of the snowmobile headed out, flying past the cabins. Danny jogged over and grabbed my arm.

"Are you okay? That guy nearly hit you!"

"I'm fine. Just soaking wet. I think I kept the towels dry."

Danny looked after the sled, his face mottled red.

"I can't believe he laughed. What kind of person does that? Let's get you back to your cabin so you can change. Geez, that guy was just a..."

"It's okay, Danny. He probably didn't mean it. Did you see who it was?"

"It looked like an older guy, but it's hard to tell when they're all bundled up. I didn't even catch the plate number on the sled. Dang it."

We kept walking and made it to my cabin without further incident. I wished I'd had time to prepare Luna for another visitor, but she seemed to take it all in stride, proudly displaying her litter. All three kittens were snuggled by her side.

"Oh, that's just too cute," Danny said. "Charlie's gonna love this. Can you tell what they are yet?"

"Not yet," I said, waving to Jasper on the bed. "I'm going to go get changed."

"I'll put the playpen over there. I like what you've done with the place, by the way."

I rolled my eyes as I grabbed a pair of jeans and a hoodie. I had done exactly nothing to the cabin, but Danny's snark reminded me I probably should. By the time I was done getting changed, he was sitting down next to Luna, a smile on his face as he watched the kits crawl around.

"I gotta go check with Carl and make sure he's got the plows and snowblowers ready. Thanks for letting me see the kittens. Bye everyone."

Once he left, I looked at Luna, but didn't move her. She was sleeping peacefully and from the looks of it, she needed her rest. Jasper hopped off the bed and inspected the playpen.

"Looks nice. That will keep the kits very safe."

"I hope so. I'm sure glad you're not out and about there. Those snowmobilers seem to delight in speeding around."

"Hopefully, all the cats will hunker down. I plan to take another nap."

Jasper stretched and nimbly jumped back onto the bed, snuggling next to my pillow. I cast one more look around the cabin before flipping off the light and heading back to the lodge. From the state of the parking lot, Wendy had her hands full again. I picked up the pace, counting down the hours until I could be back in my cabin with the cats, away from all the hustle and bustle.

Chapter Five

Dinner in the dining hall was a subdued affair. Typically, we'd be joking around, glad to be done for the day. Tonight, we sat, silenced by exhaustion, barely speaking as we pushed food around our plates. Even Danny, ever irrepressible, was strangely quiet, and never even attempted to kidnap Charlie's baked potato.

"Well, this just sucks," Charlie said, letting out a loud raspberry. "I sure hope our entire weekend won't be like this."

I forked a little roast beef into my mouth and nodded.

"I think we're all just tired. Thanks for coming in early to help. I've never seen this place get so crazy."

"No worries. With all the noise in the parking lot, I couldn't sleep. Hopefully, I'll be able to catch a catnap tonight when things slow down and Penny isn't around."

Charlie tossed a worried look over her shoulder, checking to make sure Penny wasn't close enough to hear her. Her shoulders relaxed, and she tucked into her food with more relish.

"Wedding season can get a little crazy," Danny said, pushing his empty tray forward on the table. "Especially when there are big families all staying here, but this takes the cake. Ooh, speaking of cake..."

He cast a hopeful eye towards the desert section of the buffet. The kitchen crew was working overtime to keep everyone fed, but the food was delicious, as always. Danny picked up his tray and headed over to snag some desserts. He was on his way back when I heard shouting outside.

"What's going on out there?"

Charlie beat me to the windows and let out a squeal.

"Fight!"

We streamed outside the dining hall and I instantly regretted leaving my coat on the back of my chair as the wind whipped past, scattering snowflakes everywhere. I was just about to turn back when I heard the unmistakable sound of a fist hitting flesh.

"You're going to regret that, you lowlife."

I recognized Edgar's voice as I squinted through the snow, trying to make out the figures standing a few feet away.

"Come on, we've got to get closer. Somebody better call Trevor and get him over here. This could get nasty," Charlie said, hauling me forward.

Danny pulled out his cellphone as we came to a stop a few feet away from the cluster of snowmobilers standing in the parking lot. I spotted Edgar, whose cheek had a bright red welt, backed by his friend Jim and a handful of the men who'd been the first to arrive at the resort.

Mark Chesney was squared up, handsome face flushed as he glared at the older man.

"No one calls me a cheater and gets away with it," he said around clenched teeth. "You take that back, old man. Every race I've won has been on the up and up, which is more than I can say for you."

"What?" Edgar roared, rushing forward like a bull.

Mark easily sidestepped, and Edgar slipped, hitting the pavement hard on one knee. Even though I didn't like the man, I winced. That had to hurt.

"You heard me. I never cheat, even though you do. You just can't handle the fact that I'm a better driver than you'll ever be."

Charlie stood up on her toes and heaved a sigh.

"Here comes Trevor and Josh. They'll stop this. It's just like high school, when the bullies would fight in the park."

"I was homeschooled," I said, heart pounding as Edgar got back to his feet and closed the distance towards Mark. "These are grown men. Why are they fighting like this?"

Edgar limped back to Mark and jabbed a meaty, glove covered finger into the man's chest.

"No one lays hands on me, boy. If I say you're a cheater, you're a cheater. I'm the best driver around and somehow, I've never been able to win a race when you enter. I've had it up to here with your tricks. If you're not careful, someone's gonna make sure you never compete again."

"Alright everyone, that's enough. We've been through this before," Trevor Kent, our head of security, said as he approached. "We're all adults here and we can use our words, not our fists."

Trevor's bear-like bulk seemed to deflate most of the men, but Edgar refused to back down.

"Talk is cheap," Edgar said, spitting at Mark's feet. "Sometimes, you've got to settle things like men. I'm warning you, Chesney. Your days are numbered."

Mark stood, arms folded across his chest, and shook his head.

"You can posture all you want, Edgar. We'll all know it's the whiskey talking. We'll settle this like men tomorrow at the race. I've beaten you before, and I'll do it again. Fairly. Maybe if you didn't drink so much, you'd be a better driver."

He pushed past the older man, driving his shoulder hard into Edgar, who slipped, gripping his shoulder. His face flushed to a red so dark it bordered on purple as he watched Mark walk back to the lodge.

"You'll pay for that! Just you wait!"

"Alright, Edgar, that's enough," Trevor said, heaving a sigh before taking Edgar's arm. "Every year you two fight. Don't you ever tire of it?"

"He struck me first," Edgar said, his tone edging into a whine. "Why aren't you doing anything about that? I'm a paying guest."

"And so is he. I know you drove him to it, just like you always do.

Now, let's go back inside and get you settled into your room. Show's over everyone."

Josh flanked them, gripping Edgar's other arm as they frog marched the yelling man back into the lodge. I shivered as another gust of wind sprayed me with snow. Edgar's friends muttered amongst themselves, and I caught their words as they turned away.

"Someone's gotta do something about Chesney."

"You're telling me, brother. Let's go have another beer."

I shivered again, but this time it wasn't from the cold. There was something ugly about their tone and I didn't like it. Charlie wrapped an arm around me and led me back to the dining hall.

"Don't worry about it, Eden. They always fight like this. It means nothing. It's a combination of too much testosterone and alcohol."

"I don't know, Charlie. I don't like it. I'd better go feed the cats before the snow gets any worse."

She followed me over to the buffet station where Luke was feverishly cleaning up. His face was flushed and his hazel eyes looked worried as they met mine.

"What's wrong, Luke?"

"I've got to stay late tonight. We've got a ton of prep to do for breakfast tomorrow, and Iris asked everyone to pitch in. I saved a bunch of food for the cats, but I don't think you'll be able to carry it all by yourself."

"It's okay, Luke. I can always make two trips if I need to," I said, smiling in the hopes it would break the nervous tension visible on his face.

Charlie looked at her watch and shrugged.

"I'll go with you. Danny said you took in some kittens. Maybe I can see them before I go back to work. Some cute kittens will definitely make up for that scene outside."

Luke relaxed and nodded.

"I didn't think of that. I'll go get the trays, Eden. Back in a flash."

He tossed his white rag on the buffet table and rushed back into the kitchen, gangly limbs flying.

"Thanks, Charlie. I appreciate the help. You'll love the kittens. They're so tiny! I've never seen newborns."

"Awe, they sound adorable. I'll go grab our coats. Danny already took care of our trays."

I rubbed my arms as the dreadful shivery feeling faded from my limbs. Maybe Charlie was right, and I was being too much of a worrywart. Even though we'd been several feet away from the snow-mobilers, I could smell the whiskey on their breath. It was probably all just talk, like she said.

By the time we were all bundled up, Luke reappeared, carrying a tray heaped high with leftover roast beef. Iris and the crew had been extra generous.

"Wow, that's a lot of food," Charlie said, eyes wide. "Can they eat all of that?"

"You'd be surprised," Luke said with a chuckle. "That tuxedo cat, the one Eden calls Ollie, he'd probably eat half this tray by himself if the other cats let him. I've got one more. I'll be right back."

He returned with a smaller tray laden with corn and potatoes. I smiled, knowing that a few of the cats would be thrilled. I'd never known cats enjoyed vegetables until I met the clowder. Corn was a big favorite among a few of the cats. Even Fig enjoyed it, although she'd never admit it. I took the smaller tray while Charlie hefted the bigger one and we headed outside.

"Brrr. How cold is it supposed to get tonight?"

I just barely heard her voice over the howling wind and moved closer.

"I think down into the teens. I'm glad the kitchen put aside extra for the cats. I hate to think of them being cold."

We plowed through the newly fallen snow that was quickly piling up in silence. The walk, that usually took just about five minutes, seemed to drag on for hours until we finally approached the clearing.

Charlie put down the tray and stretched her back, wincing.

"Oof, that was longer than it looked. So, what do we do now? Do we just leave it here?"

"We usually feed them right over there. I'll go brush the snow off the tray we use. They'll show up in a few minutes."

I got everything ready for the cats and sure enough, one by one, I could see their eyes as they approached. Fig was in the lead, but she pulled up when she spotted Charlie.

"Who's this?"

I dropped into a crouch and motioned for Charlie to do the same. She knew I talked to Jasper, but she didn't know it was a two-way street.

"They're not used to you, Charlie," I said, making eye contact with Fig. "Once they know you're my friend and you won't hurt them, they'll relax."

Ollie bounded forward, spraying snow, as he spotted the tray of roast beef. A sharp yowl from Fig brought him up short, and he hung his head.

"Oh, how cute is he?" Charlie said, squealing before she lowered her voice. "I love his coat."

The younger cats approached first, as usual, and ate their fill of the meat before stepping aside. Charlie watched in wonder as the clowder made quick work of the food we'd brought. I spotted Benny hanging back, and my heart sank. I could hear his breathing from where we were sitting. I noticed the other cats left a portion for him and once they were done, Fig waved her tail and he approached slowly, never taking his eyes off us.

The brown cat moved a safe distance away and nodded at me, blinking her eyes in a silent thank you. The cats melted into the trees, leaving Benny to enjoy his meal.

"Is he okay? Why didn't he eat with the others?" Charlie asked.

"He's sick. I tried to catch him earlier, but he ran away. I don't want to scare him now and have him miss out on his meal."

Charlie's eyes misted as we watched the thin cat methodically eat his food, coughing every few bites.

"Oh, the poor thing. Isn't there anything we can do for him?"

"I'll try again," I said, not wanting to tip Benny off to my plans. "He's almost done."

I stood up and Benny hissed, scattering the snow in front of the tray. Charlie called out to him.

"It's okay, kitty. We won't hurt you."

He stopped at her voice and stood, one paw in the air. I moved a little closer, and he hissed, before giving her another long look and disappearing into the trees. My shoulders slumped.

"He seemed to like your voice. Maybe you can come with me tomorrow and we'll try again."

"I never realized how cool these cats are," Charlie said, grabbing the trays and handing me one. "I'll definitely come back with you. That sick cat reminded me of one I had when I was little. He had a black nose, just like that. I named him Benjamin. He was such a wonderful cat. It broke my heart when he got out. I never knew what happened to him. It was years and years ago. I was probably five."

I blinked, surprised. Was it a coincidence the sick cat's name was Benny? There was no way it was the same cat. Was there?

"That's a cute name."

"I called him that because he was as cute as a button with that little black nose. I'd better get back to the desk so Wendy can go home. I'm sure she's exhausted."

We walked back with our now empty trays and I noticed the snow had already filled in our tracks. It was going to be difficult to get back to the cats tomorrow, but I'd make it. With any luck, I'd be able to capture Benny and get him to the vet.

We were almost at the dining hall when the roar of an engine deafened me. A snowmobile shot past, spraying us with snow. Seconds later, another one raced after it. We turned and watched their headlights as they roared towards the forest. My heart clenched painfully as I imagined the cats running in fear.

"Somebody needs to put a stop to this," Charlie said, wiping the snow off her face. "They've gone too far."

I silently agreed with her as we trudged through the snow again. I was thoroughly sick of getting sprayed with snow and I couldn't shake the dread creeping up my spine.

Chapter Six

Sometime later, in the deep dark of night, a horrible yowl outside my cabin yanked me from a disturbing dream. I blinked, making out Jasper cuddled next to my feet. His eyes were open and his ears trained on the door.

"What was that?"

"It's Oscar. You'd better let him in. That wind sounds terrible."

I tossed off my blankets and winced as my feet hit the chilly floor. A quick glance at my watch revealed it was just a little after three. I sighed as I opened the door, revealing a cat covered in snow.

"Oh my goodness, Oscar. Come in. You're nearly white with all that snow over you."

He grabbed something at his feet and marched into my cabin, tail held high. A sleepy meow sounded from the corner where Luna was tucked in with her kittens.

"Oscar, is that you?"

I flipped on the light and nearly screamed when I saw the giant rat in his mouth. Was it my imagination or was it still moving? He dropped it in front of Luna and sat down, chest puffed out.

"Fig said you'd be here, and I wanted to make sure you and our kits had plenty of food. I want my kits to be hunters, not sissified house cats who rely on humans for food."

He shook his fur, depositing snow all over my floors as I shot a look at Jasper to see how he took the younger cat's comments. His whiskers were quirked in a kitty grin.

"I sense an insult, lightly buried."

Oscar blanched as much as a cat as dark as night could and whipped his head towards the former leader of his clowder.

"I meant no offense. It's only... Well, these are my first kits."

"I know." Jasper jumped off the bed and stalking over. "You have much to learn. Including the proper seasons in which to have kittens without risking their lives and the lives of their mother."

Oscar's head dipped and an awkward silence filled the room. Luna sighed deeply and placed a paw on the rat. I was pretty sure it was dead. I sure hoped so.

"Thank you for thinking of us. Eden has been taking wonderful care of us and I'm certain once the babies are a little older, they'll learn much from Jasper if he doesn't mind teaching them."

Jasper's chest puffed out and a new light came into his eyes. I turned my head away so they wouldn't see me smile.

"Wait, this is only temporary, right? Just until the storm gets better and the men leave. You're not seriously thinking of raising our kits in a house?"

Oscar bristled as he looked around the room, fur fluffed. Jasper shook his head before gently sniffing Luna and giving her a quick lick on the forehead.

"They will stay as long as necessary to ensure their safety. It's too cold out there for kits, and you know it. Eden has been gracious enough to offer to share her home, and you should be grateful instead of rude."

Oscar's startling blue eyes swept past mine and I was surprised to see anger in their depths. He quickly broke eye contact and nodded towards Jasper.

"Of course. I will still hunt for you, my love," he said, looking at Luna with fierceness. "I should get back to the clowder. I'll come back later."

He swept past me and strode to the door, scratching at it with his long, sharp claws. I hurried before he could do any damage to the wooden surface.

"If I'm here, I'll open the door for you, but you should know I'm usually at work during the daylight hours. I'll check on them as often as I can."

Oscar's eyes narrowed, and a chill went through me as I realized how little he liked me.

"This is only temporary, Eden. Don't forget that. Soon, my kits will be back in the wild, where they belong."

Luna's secret wish to have the girl kitten live a different life reared its head again, but I knew this wasn't the time to bring it up.

"Well, until then, I'll do what I can to keep them safe."

We were at an impasse and Oscar knew it. His lip curled, revealing a gleaming ivory fang, and he glanced towards the trees.

"I wish you could make yourself useful and do something about the men. Two of them were far too close to the clowder tonight. Their shouting disturbed everyone."

He shook the moisture off his coat and leapt away, his dark form quickly vanishing from sight. I stood in the doorway for a moment, watching him go, and wondered what he meant. Men shouting near the clowder? That seemed odd. Everything was silent now, so whoever it was must have given up and packed it in. I shivered and stepped back inside, closing the door firmly.

The sound of chomping coming from Luna's direction made my stomach weak as I realized Luna was making quick work of Oscar's gift. I was definitely going to need to give that bed a thorough cleaning. Jasper's whiskers quirked again before he headed to the bed and hopped up, making himself comfortable.

I flipped off the light and snuggled under the covers, trying to get warm. I was certain the odds of my falling asleep again were slim to none, but I drifted off almost instantly, dreaming of men shouting, cats fighting, and tiny kittens watching it all with sad eyes.

My alarm sounded all too soon, and I woke up cross, the unsettled feeling from my dreams following me into the waking world. I checked on Luna and the kittens, all sleeping soundly, and Jasper, also sleeping soundly, and got ready as quietly as I could. It was still dark out and I figured I'd be one of the first employees at the dining hall for breakfast. I wouldn't mind a little extra peace.

Once I was dressed, I made sure everyone had plenty of food and water before bundling up. I paused at the door and turned back to give Jasper a kiss between his little ears.

His little mrrp of pleasure chased away my bad mood and by the time I made it to the dining hall, I was smiling, even though the snow was up to my knees. Carl was snow blowing a path from the dining hall to the lodge and nodded as I pushed open the doors. The hive of activity surprised me as I spotted all the kitchen workers running back and forth, packing boxes of food like crazy. Iris came by, her face flushed, and nodded.

"Morning, Eden. We'll have the buffet ready for the employees shortly. We've just got to finish all these takeout orders for the guests."

"No worries. I'm not in a rush. Is there anything I can do to help?"

She stopped and blinked in surprise before nodding.

"You can help Luke sort the boxes. That would be super helpful. Thanks, Eden."

I headed toward the station where Luke was surrounded by white to-go boxes. I waited until he finished creating a stack before speaking up so I wouldn't throw him off.

"Hi, Luke. Can I help?"

"Oh, hi, Eden. Sure. Here comes Amber with more orders. We need to separate everything. So, this stack here is for biscuits and gravy. This one is for omelets, and this one is for pancake breakfasts."

"Sure!"

We worked in companionable silence until everything was sorted. An almost audible sigh of relief swept through the hall as everyone finished up their duties.

"Great work, everyone," Iris said, mopping her brow with a dish rag. "Let's finish getting the employee breakfast buffet ready while Luke runs these over to the lodge."

Everyone dispersed and Iris joined us, patting me on the arm.

"Nice of you to pitch in. We made those little French toast rolls you love so much this morning. I'll make sure you get extra."

"Thank you, Iris. Luke, I can help carry these across if it will save time. We're setting everything up in the hall, right?"

"Yep, we've got the warmers already going," Iris confirmed. "You're a gem, Eden."

Luke packed everything into special insulated bags and we each took as many as we could carry, leaving only three bags behind. Amber smiled at Luke, her face flushing a little as she made eye contact.

"I can get those."

I bit my lip to hide my smile and followed the pair outside. Amber had started two weeks ago, and it was clear the shy girl was interested in Luke. I didn't know her well, but she seemed nice. I hustled to catch up with her, mentally thanking Carl for doing such a good job on the snow removal. This wouldn't have been fun wading through a few feet of snow.

"Are you liking it here, Amber?"

She glanced over at me and I noticed for the first time her eyes were a lovely shade of pale blue-gray.

"I am. Everyone here is pretty nice. Iris is a good boss."

"She is," I said, nodding. "You don't live here on site? I don't think I've seen you in the cabins?"

"No, I've still got a few months left on my apartment lease, so I drive in from Greenville every day."

"Oof, that's a long drive. The cabins are really nice. Hopefully, you can make the switch once your lease is up."

She glanced ahead at Luke's back and blushed.

"Yeah, maybe."

We headed inside and I relished the blast of warm air as we walked into the lobby. Charlie popped her head up from behind the desk and grinned before blowing an enormous bubble with her gum.

"Well, this is a surprise. Here, let me help. I heard Penny's crew getting the tables set up in there earlier. She said Iris should've been in charge of that."

"Imagine that, Penny complaining about something."

I glanced around to make sure the ever-present Penny hadn't overheard me and relaxed a little. Charlie grabbed a bag off my shoulder and led the way into the ballroom area. Luke began stacking everything under the warming lights and Amber rushed to lend a hand. I stepped back to leave them to it, noticing they were carrying on a hushed conversation.

"Anything exciting happen last night?" I asked Charlie.

"Just a few noisy snowmobilers whooping it up, but they finally quit a little after one. I heard a few side doors open and shut after that, but nobody came up to the front desk. Good thing, too. I just downloaded a new book, and it was so good I didn't want to put it down."

"Well, thank goodness there weren't any more fights."

Luke and Amber finished arranging everything and gathered up the transport bags. Luke bobbed his head at me.

"Breakfast should be ready in about fifteen minutes. Thanks again for your help!"

"See you guys later," I said, waving as the couple headed out. Charlie and I walked back to the front desk where a man was standing, looking around. Charlie rushed ahead, her ponytail swaying back and forth.

"Good morning. Do you need anything?"

The man was a little older than us and was part of the group that checked in at the normal time the day before. He'd been pleasant and undemanding then, but it was clear he was definitely worried about something now.

"Oh, thank goodness. I didn't know who to call. Mark, our team leader, isn't answering his door and I'm worried about him. He specifically asked us to get up early to get some practice in."

"Mark Chesney?" I asked.

"Yeah," the man said, shoving his hands into his pockets. "I'm his mechanic. He's never late or I wouldn't be so worried. He runs a tight ship."

"Did he go out early without you?"

"No, his sled is right outside. He mentioned it wasn't acting right last night, and we needed to check everything over. He's not responding to texts or calls. Do you think you could let me borrow his room key to check on him?"

Charlie and I traded glances and a thread of worry shot through my stomach as I remembered the fight between Mark and Edgar the night before. She shook her head and the man's shoulders bunched.

"I'm sorry, we can't do that. Are you certain he's not just somewhere on the grounds?"

"I'm positive. Mark never pulls stunts like this. He's one of the most professional drivers I've ever worked with."

The doors slid open and Trevor came in, stomping the snow off his boots. I touched Charlie's arm and waved him down.

"Trevor! Would you mind helping us for a second? This guy, I'm sorry, what was your name?"

"Dave. Dave Shepherd."

"Dave's looking for Mark Chesney and says he's not answering his phone. Could you go with us to do a wellness check in Mark's room?"

Trevor nodded at Dave and reached over to shake his hand.

"I remember you from last year. You're Mark's mechanic, right?"

"Yep. I'm sorry to cause a bunch of drama, but this really isn't like Mark at all. If we could just check his room, I'd feel a lot better. Maybe he just overslept, but I have this feeling..."

Dave trailed off and Trevor's forehead bunched into lines. He nodded at Charlie.

"I'll take him up and use my security override card. You ladies stay here."

He led Dave towards the elevators, and I waited until the doors closed before I turned to Charlie.

"You don't think?"

"I sure hope not. You heard what Edgar was saying last night. He was really mad."

I tapped my fingers on the desk and stared at the elevators, hoping Mark really had just slept in. After what felt like an eternity, the lights flashed and the elevator fired up, coming back down to the lobby. I held my breath as the doors slid open, revealing Dave and Trevor. Neither man looked happy, and my heart sank.

"I'll go check the cameras and see if Mark was seen leaving the lodge this morning. We'll track him down, Dave."

An awful thought occurred to me as I suddenly remembered what Oscar had said the night before. I had a sinking suspicion I knew where Mark was, but how could I bring it up? I couldn't exactly say a cat told me about an argument in the forest in the middle of the night.

"You know, I was up early this morning and heard a ruckus in the forest. Maybe we could check it out."

Trevor's eyes narrowed as he searched my face.

"What time?"

"Three-ish. I can lead someone there, but it's going to be hard going with all this snow."

"I shouldn't use Mark's sled, but we have a back-up sled in the trailer. I'll go get it ready. You're certain?"

I nodded as Dave sprinted out of the lobby. Trevor and Charlie leaned close to me.

"You know something, don't you?" Trevor asked.

"Maybe. I definitely heard something that sounded like shout-ing. I have a bad feeling about this, guys."

"I'll grab the lodge's sled and you can ride along. I have the same feeling."

I shoved my hands deep into my pockets and hoped I was wrong and I'd be leading everyone on a fruitless mission. The alternative was something I wasn't ready to think about.

Chapter Seven

The cold air whipping past my face took my breath away as I hunkered down behind Trevor on the sled. I'd never been on a snowmobile before and if this was any sign of what riding one was like, I wasn't in any hurry to repeat it.

"How much further?"

Trevor's voice was barely audible over the engine, but I risked peeking out behind his broad back and pointed to the right.

"Just up there a little way."

We shot ahead, and I said a quick prayer that the clowder cats were all safely tucked up in their dens. Trevor came to a stop about five hundred yards from where I'd been the day before and cut the engine. I got off the sled with shaky legs and looked around.

The trees weren't as thick here, but there was no sign of anyone around, alive or dead. I breathed a sigh of relief. Maybe whatever Oscar heard had just been an argument and nothing sinister. Dave pulled in behind us and looked around as Trevor got off his sled. His beard was encrusted with snow and I was suddenly very glad I'd been sheltering behind him. People actually did this for fun? I huddled into my coat and breathed out, watching the steam from my breath.

"Are you sure it's around here? How could you tell from your cabin?" Trevor asked, raising a brow.

I nodded and looked around.

"Maybe not exactly right here, but the shouting was definitely coming from this direction. Maybe we should look around on foot."

Dave put his hands on his hips and looked at the ground.

"There's no sign of any sled tracks, but that was one heck of a storm last night. They might have filled in already."

A flicker of movement caught my eye, and I immediately spotted Willow's mottled coat in the snow. She lashed her tail and darted behind a tree. Uh oh. I started in her direction.

"I'll look over here if you want to fan out. Hopefully, I was wrong, and it was just the wind playing tricks with the sounds."

I hurried after Willow and nearly tripped over her as I passed a snow encrusted shrub. She shied away, eyes wide, and checked behind me.

"You're alone?"

"I am," I said, talking as quietly as I could. "What's up?"

"There's something over here. This morning, I heard Oscar complaining to Fig about men shouting in the night and went to check it out. At first, I thought he was just trying to distract her from the reason he left last night, but I wasn't sure. I need to get back to my hunting party, but when I saw you, I thought I'd help. I can smell something bad over this way."

She leapt over a snowdrift and led the way, while I followed at a much slower pace, nearly coming to my knees in the deep snow. I saw what looked like tracks and carefully avoided them. We were getting closer.

I was breathing hard by the time Willow came to a stop, a sad look on her little face.

"He's just ahead. I knew when I smelled death, it wasn't good. Do you think he froze to death?"

I risked a few steps more and gasped as I saw what she was looking at. There, stretched out on top of a snow bank, was Mark Chesney. His skin was a bluish white color, and I knew we'd found him too late. The look on his face made me turn away, and I was suddenly glad I hadn't eaten yet.

"Thanks, Willow. I'll let the guys know. I'm afraid this place is going to be crawling with people for a few days. You'll have to let Fig know so everyone can avoid this area until they're done."

She nodded before brushing past, wrapping her tail around my leg.

"I don't understand humans. Why would he come all this way on foot? Who was yelling at him? Do you think he was killed? When cats have a problem, they work it out, only resorting to tooth and claw if it's absolutely necessary."

"I know, sweetheart. Does everyone have enough to eat? It's so cold. I can bring more food later."

"We're fine. Once you get moving, it's not too bad. Thanks, Eden. I'm sorry about whoever that was. No one should meet their end alone like that."

In a flash, she was gone, leaving me to look at Mark's body. I inched closer and tried to look at the scene analytically. There was no blood. Did that mean he'd been strangled? I didn't want to touch the body, but it was impossible to tell if he'd been shot or stabbed, especially since he was wearing a thick puffer coat.

He was arranged oddly, almost like he was sleeping. Whoever had dragged him out here went to the trouble of arranging his arms over his body. That was definitely weird.

I was just about to sneak behind the body when the sound of someone breathing heavily nearby made me freeze in my tracks. Was someone here? Had they heard me talking to Willow?

"Hello?"

The sound cut off, and I looked around, trying to figure out where it had come from. Movement under a shrub caught my eye, and I saw Benny, the black portions of his fur, standing out sharply against the snow. He coughed, and I took a step towards him.

"Benny? Are you okay?"

He coughed again before his eyes flared wide and he looked behind me.

"Eden?"

I turned to see Trevor a few yards off and by the time I looked back, Benny was gone. Dang it. What if he'd witnessed what happened here? I sighed and called out to Trevor.

"Over here. I found him. I was just going to call over to you."

His heavy steps crunched through the snow and I held up a hand.

"Be careful! There are some tracks the police might need. I should call Ethan."

"No cell service out here. Are you sure it's him? He's dead?"

"I'm certain."

He let out a colorful curse as he crouched down near the body, shaking his head.

"I thought I heard you talking to someone when I was walking this way," Trevor said, his eyes wary.

"I spotted one of the clowder cats," I said. "It's a sick one who's been staying on the fringes. He ran off, though."

"I wish he could talk. He might have been able to tell us what happened. I'm sorry you had to see this, Eden. Poor Mark. He was always a pretty good dude. I'll have to tell Dave. He's going to take it hard. It looks like he came out here, got turned around in the dark, and froze to death. What was he thinking?"

"I don't think he froze to death, Trevor," I said, risking another look at Mark's face. "I think he was killed. Look at his expression. Whatever he saw before his death terrified him."

Trevor said an even more colorful curse and looked around.

"Are you sure?"

"You heard Edgar last night. He threatened him in front of everyone. It doesn't look good. I heard shouting, and we found Mark right where I thought it came from. I don't think he came out here alone and shouted before lying down to die. He was an experienced snowmobiler and probably knew a lot about winter survival. I just don't see him freezing to death."

"Well, shoot. I'll mark the area and we'll head back until we get service. This won't look good for the resort or my security team."

"You found him! Is he okay?"

I winced as Dave burst into the clearing, walking right over the tracks I'd wanted to preserve.

"Dave, stop! You're trampling on evidence."

Dave's face fell as he saw Mark's body and he plowed ahead, further obliterating the tracks. Why didn't I take a picture?

"Come on, buddy. You've gotta get up. The race is later today and we need to get your sled tuned up. Mark?"

I exchanged a glance with Trevor, and suspicion crept into my heart as I watched Dave shake Mark's body. It was extremely clear Mark was dead. What was wrong with Dave? Had he intentionally disrupted the tracks in the snow?

Trevor pulled Dave off and shook him by the shoulders.

"He's dead, man. I'm sorry, but this is a crime scene. We need to notify the authorities."

"This can't be happening. It just can't. There's some sort of mistake. He's playing a joke on us or something. He can't be dead. He said..."

"What did he say?" I asked, breaking in as Dave trailed off.

"Nothing. It's not important. I just don't believe it. Mark Chesney was bigger than life. He took chances no one else would take, and he always came out on top."

Dave trailed off again, but his meaning was clear. Except this time. Someone had ended Mark's life. Trevor led the way back to the sled, and my mind raced. Edgar was the most obvious choice, but was it too obvious? Dave was acting strangely. There was something about him that seemed familiar, but I knew we'd never met before this weekend. I pulled my hood up over my ears to block the wind and kept trudging through the snow.

"Do you think you can find this spot again?" Trevor asked, his face pale behind his beard.

"I think so, but it wouldn't hurt to mark it, just in case."

"Let me see what I've got in here."

Trevor rummaged around in the box attached to the lodge's sled and let out a shout.

"I've got some spray paint. I'll spray an arrow right here and then we'll try to find a place with some service."

I huddled in my coat, waiting, while trying to watch Dave without being too obvious. He stood, staring back into the trees, his greyish eyes blank.

"How did he get here? It's a long walk from the lodge. I just don't see him doing that, especially late at night. He was always an early to bed kind of guy. He said it helped him keep his competitive edge."

"Have you heard anything from the other teams? He had a pretty public fight last night outside with Edgar. I don't think I saw you with everyone."

Dave startled, almost like he'd forgotten I was there, and his cheeks reddened.

"Oh. I was in the trailer, working on the sleds. We've had some weird issues with them lately."

"Sabotage?"

"Well, I mean..."

He clammed up as Trevor came plowing back through the snow. Interesting.

"Alright, let's head back. Once we're closer to the lodge, we should have a signal. I know you know Ethan, but it's best if we call 9-1-1."

I nodded and got back on the sled, wishing I was tucked inside my cozy cabin. This was not how I'd imagined my day starting. The sled lurched forward, and I grabbed Trevor's waist to keep from falling off. He roared ahead, and I lowered my head, wishing heartily that winter was over.

Halfway back to the lodge, we stopped, and Trevor placed the call to the police. While he was busy, I pulled out my phone and sent a text to Ethan, figuring it wouldn't hurt. The sled lurched forward again, and I nearly dropped my phone in the snow before sliding it into my pocket.

I glanced back over my shoulder towards the trees as questions swirled in my mind. I didn't believe Mark would've willingly gone with someone into the woods in the middle of the night. There was no blood around his body. Had he been killed at the resort and moved? I shook my head as we came to a stop in front of the lodge.

It was clear someone had hated Mark Chesney enough to kill him. Edgar was the likeliest suspect, but if the past few months had taught me anything, it could be anyone. There was a murderer staying at the Valewood Resort, and I was determined to catch them.

Chapter Eight

C onsidering the way yesterday started, let alone the way today was going, I was expecting chaos when I walked into the lobby, but a deep hush, broken only by Charlie's welcome, greeted me.

"Eden! What's going on? Did you find him?"

I shook my head slightly as Dave entered behind me, looking lost. My heart, even though I had questions about his innocence, went out to him. I put a hand on his arm.

"Dave, you can wait for the police in the lounge, or if you're hungry, there's food in the ballroom.

His eyes were filled with raw emotion as he stared at me and, for a moment, I wondered if he heard me.

"I can't eat at a time like this. Mark is dead! Don't you understand?"

He pushed past me and headed towards the elevators, punching the button angrily. I bit my lip and slid off my hat before walking behind the desk. Charlie's face was frozen in shock as I hung up my coat.

"You found him?"

Her voice, although quiet, seemed to ring through the empty

lobby. I nodded and heaved a gigantic sigh before leaning against the desk, burying my head in my hands.

"We did. It's not good, Charlie. It looks like he was murdered."

Trevor walked in, his bearded face grim as he headed in our direction. He looked around before leaning across the desk.

"The word is going to get out, but let's keep this quiet for as long as we can. The police will be here soon. Have you called Mr. Marsburg?"

"No, not yet. Dave went up to his room. Well, at least I think he did. He took the elevator. Trevor..."

"We have to make sure no one leaves the resort until the police lock it down. I'll hang out here to help. Charlie, is Josh still in the security room?"

"I think so. He hasn't left, and it's just a little before shift change," she said, glancing at the clock in front of the desk. "I can stay on if that will help."

Trevor nodded.

"That would be great. Eden, you can call the boss man, and I'll get Josh to pull up all the security feeds from last night. When the cops come, I'll take them out to the site. You don't need to see that again."

Mark's tortured face flashed in front of my eyes and my hands shook as I dialed Marsburg's number. After everything that happened just a few short weeks ago, he wouldn't appreciate this. The phone rang several times before going to voicemail. I left a brief message and hung up the phone, twisting my hands together as sirens sounded in the distance.

"Did you let Ethan know?"

I turned to Charlie and nodded before realizing my cell phone was still in my coat pocket. I walked over to grab it, noticing that although my text to Ethan was marked as read, he hadn't replied. My stomach twisted.

"I just can't believe this is happening again."

Charlie looked around and lowered her head.

"I know. I mean, there was a murder before I started working here, but the past few months have been crazy. Are we cursed?"

A shiver worked its way down my spine, but I tried to shake it off. Flashing lights from the police cars in the parking lot took my mind off her question and I stood on my tiptoes, hoping to get a glimpse of Ethan. Right now, his cool-headedness would come very much in handy.

Trevor walked outside to greet them and I gripped the desk, my knuckles turning white. Charlie patted my back, her face troubled.

"I feel the same way. I know I'm innocent, but whenever I see the cops, I always feel like I'm guilty."

Movement outside drew my attention, and I spotted Detective Ethan Rhodes as he approached Trevor, bundled up against the cold. He walked by the window in front of the desk, and my heart twinged as he looked inside, meeting my eyes. His freckled face, typically so friendly, looked hard. I watched as Trevor pointed towards the forest and wished the glass wasn't so thick so I could hear what was being said.

He got on the back of the sled and roared off with Trevor, not glancing inside again. The elevators pinged and three men got out. Edgar was in the lead, his face flushed as he laughed uproariously at something his friend said. He slapped the desk with a meaty hand and I shuddered again, thinking that his hands might have been the weapons that ended Mark Chesney's life.

"What's going on out there? Why are the cops here?"

I searched his face, hoping to spot a flicker of guilt, something that would incriminate him in Mark's murder, but I saw only the eyes of a man with a terrible hangover. They were threaded liberally with red and sunken into his fleshy cheeks. Dark circles stood out against the pallor of his face.

"It's a resort matter," Charlie said, jumping into the conversation. "There is breakfast in the ballroom, but we're asking all guests to remain in the lodge for the moment."

"What? You've gotta be kidding me," Edgar shouted, his voice so loud it made my ears hurt. "We've got practice and then a race. What the hell is going on? Is this one of Mark's tricks? He thinks he can keep us cooped up here so we can't compete?"

Again, I watched his face for any sign of guilt, but came up empty. His face, now flushed bright red, was twisted into irritation. Charlie glanced at me before her hand slowly went underneath the desk. I nodded slightly, and she pushed the button that would alert Josh to come up to the front. Edgar was violent, and if he wanted to get past us, it would only take a swipe of one of his powerful arms to send Charlie and me flying.

"I'm sorry, but we can't go into any details. Right now, all guests need to stay inside the lodge for their own safety. If you head to the ballroom, you'll find breakfast ready for you."

Edgar turned to his friends and put his hands on his hips.

"Are you hearing this? I can't believe it."

One man, Jim, if I remembered correctly, shook his head.

"It's alright, Edgar. Let's get something to eat. I'm sure it's only going to be for a few minutes. Let these ladies work."

He shot me an apologetic half-smile, which made Edgar even madder.

"Oh, come on, don't you see what's happening? I knew Mark was a cheater, but I didn't think he'd stoop this low. This resort is probably part of his plan. Next year, we're staying somewhere else. I don't care how good a deal they give us to stay here."

Josh appeared and strode towards the men, his wide shoulders blocking them from our view.

"Gentleman, is there a problem here?"

Charlie and I peeked around Josh's back.

"Oh, for pete's sake," Edgar said, grumbling. "Let's go get some grub boys. Maybe by then these people will get their acts together."

He stabbed a finger in my direction as he walked past.

"I'm not done with you. Your boss will hear about your sassy attitude. I swear, I young people think you run the world and like to throw your weight around. You'll see what happens. And look at her hair," he said, pointing at Charlie. "It's a disgrace, that's what it is."

Josh herded the group towards the ballroom and I let out a sigh of relief as Edgar's loud rant finally was out of earshot.

"I don't like him," Charlie said, gripping my arm. "He threat-

ened you. When Ethan comes back, we need to tell him that. He's
got to be the murderer."

"I don't think he did it," I said, looking down the hall where
Edgar had walked. "I wanted it to be him, but I don't think he's
guilty. You heard what he said. He was acting like Mark was still
alive."

She cracked her gum and shook her head.

"I don't know. He could have been acting."

"Well, if he is, he deserves an award. I was pretty convinced."

"What's going on? Why are there so many police cars outside?"

Wendy hustled behind the desk, eyes wide, and Charlie quickly
filled her in on Mark's death. Tears gathered in Wendy's eyes and
she shook her head.

"Not Mark. He was always so charming. So full of life. I can't
believe it. Was it a snowmobiling accident?"

"No," I said, lowering my voice. "He was killed."

Wendy gasped and her hand went to her neck, fiddling with her
necklace.

"No! I can't believe it. Who would do such a thing?"

I looked outside as Trevor and Ethan came roaring back into the
lot on the sled. Ethan got out and began directing the coroner's
team and the forensic crew. He glanced towards the window and
our eyes met.

"Hopefully, we'll find out quickly. Maybe the killer left some sort
of clue on the body. I didn't want to disturb any evidence, so I didn't
poke around too much."

"Another murder," Wendy said, wrapping her arms tightly
around her middle. "I just don't understand it."

The men walked into the lobby and I waved them over.

"Trevor, Edgar Hanson is in the ballroom. He was not happy
about being told to stay put. I'm not sure how much longer we can
keep them here."

Ethan nodded.

"I'll get the uniformed officers in here to help. We appreciate
you taking the initiative. Eden, Trevor says you're the one who
discovered the body. I'll need to get a statement from you and

everyone else. We're going to be here for a while. Is there a room we can use to interview everyone? I'd like to isolate people since apparently it's a sizeable group."

"Will my office work? It's a little small, but I don't want to take over Mr. Marsburg's office when he's not here. I left a message, but he hasn't answered."

"I'll try him again," Charlie said.

I led Ethan back through the hallway and opened my office door. I'd left it pretty clean, but there were a few things laying on my desk. Tension filled the room as Ethan shut the door and I busied myself picking up some notebooks.

"I'll just tidy things up," I said, wishing he'd say something. "You can use my computer if you need it. I have nothing to hide."

"Thanks for letting me use your office."

His voice was soft, but something was definitely off. Ethan and I had grown closer after he'd helped me get Charity over to her grandmother's. Since then, I'd seen little of him and I felt unsettled. Why was I thinking about this when there was a dead man on the resort grounds? Get it together, Eden!

"So, how can I help?"

"Take a seat and I'll get your statement. Trevor already filled me in on the basics, but I want to hear your version of it."

We both walked behind my desk, bumping shoulders, and I let out a laugh flavored with nervousness.

"Sorry, habit. I'll sit over here."

He sat in my office chair and I perched on the edge of the guest chair across from the desk. I'd never sat there, and I was surprised at how uncomfortably hard it was. I rarely had anyone else in my office for more than a few minutes. Maybe this was why.

"Start at the beginning."

I searched his freckled face for a moment, trying to get my bearings, and I wasn't sure I liked what I saw there. Typically, his sky-blue eyes were friendly. Today, they were flat and somehow cold. I shoved my worries aside and began outlining how I'd found Mark's body, leaving out Willow's help.

"You spend a lot of time in the woods, don't you?" Ethan asked, his tone guarded.

"I do. I look after the clowder that lives there. One cat just had kittens, and with the storm coming, I took them in to my cabin. They're the cutest little things."

"Trevor mentioned Mark was quite the ladies' man. Would you agree?"

I was thrown by the question and shrugged.

"I don't know. He seemed very nice. I'd guess you could say he was attractive, if you liked that type."

Ethan looked out the window.

"Were you in the forest last night?"

"I was. I always feed the cats after dinner time. Usually, Luke goes with me, but he was tied up in the kitchen last night, so Charlie went along. Why?"

"Did you see Mark when you were there?"

"No, I didn't. We saw two snowmobiles racing around when we were walking back, but we didn't see Mark."

"And you're certain he wasn't there?"

"Yes. I saw him walk back into the lodge after the fight and then we went to feed the cats. Wait. Do you think I killed Mark?"

"Fight? What fight?"

I was still hung up on his obvious suspicion, and an icy feeling swept through my stomach.

"Edgar Hanson and Mark got into it outside the dining hall last night. Everyone saw it. Are you seriously accusing me of killing Mark?"

He eyes met mine. This time, they were unguarded, and I was surprised by the depth of emotion in their sky-blue depths.

"I'm not. But if he attacked you and you fought back, it's self defense, Eden. I have to ask. I'm sorry."

I sat, frozen in my chair, shaking as unwanted memories rushed over me like a tidal wave. My ex-boyfriend holding me captive, Hannah Murphy, coming to my rescue before I was murdered. It took several seconds to find my voice.

"I didn't kill Mark. Charlie was with me the whole time. We fed the cats, nearly got run over by snowmobilers, and I went home. How could you think that of me?"

"Trevor thought it was strange how easily you found the body. How could you hear shouting in your cabin and know exactly where to go? I don't want to believe it, but I have to ask. You need to understand how it looks. Did someone else you know do it and you're covering for them? Please, tell me the truth."

I couldn't, though. I couldn't tell Ethan that I could talk to cats. That Oscar had shown up and described the shouting in the woods near the clowder's den. That Willow had led me to the body. I hated lying to him. It's not who I was. But how could I tell him the truth? And if I did... what were the odds he'd believe me?

Chapter Nine

W e stared at each other as I wrestled with my conscience. I needed to say something, but what? Finally, I laid as many cards on the table as I could. Some day, if I ever had the guts to tell him the truth about my ability to speak to cats, he might hate that I lied to him. But today, I wasn't ready to go there. Not yet. I closed my eyes and spoke.

"Have you ever had a feeling? An intuition that whispered something that later turned out to be true? That's the best way I can describe how I found Mark's body so quickly. I had help, too. You remember that little tortoiseshell cat that was with me when we found Charity? I spotted her in the woods and she led me right to the body. I know it sounds farfetched, but that's what happened. After that fight last night, I had a bad feeling. After I heard the shouting, it got worse."

I opened my eyes and saw Ethan staring at me, his eyes pleading with me to trust him. He sat silently, and his eyes never left mine. Finally, he broke the staring contest and looked at my desk.

"Tell me more about this fight. Why didn't someone report it to us last night? If you had, this might not have happened."

A sick feeling that he was right twisted through my stomach.

"Maybe we should have. The people who've been here the longest said it always happens. I guess the snowmobilers are super competitive and when you combine alcohol with that much testosterone, fights break out. It's not the first time the security team has had to break apart a fight."

"Describe exactly what happened."

"We heard shouting from the dining hall and when we came outside, Charlie, Danny, and me, we saw Edgar Hanson squaring off with Mark in the parking lot. It looked like Mark had just punched or slapped Edgar. His face was all red. Cheating accusations were thrown around on all sides and then Edgar rushed at Mark. He missed and hit the pavement hard on a knee. He was limping afterwards. That's odd..."

"What?"

"When I saw him this morning, he seemed fine. As irritable as ever. He wasn't limping."

"Maybe he didn't hit it that hard."

"I don't know. Anyway, that's when Trevor broke up the fight. Mark left and Edgar shouted after him he'd pay for that as security escorted him back to the lodge. As far as I know, they took him to his room to sleep it off."

"You mentioned seeing two snowmobiles while you were coming back from feeding the clowder?"

I nodded.

"Yes. They came really close and sprayed us with snow. That wasn't the first time it happened, either. I was getting really sick of it by that point."

"Did you see the plates or the color of the sleds?"

"No. It was too dark. They were both men from the sound of their laughs as they drove off. Is there something we can do to keep them from tearing around? They go through the forest and I'm worried about the cats. Are they breaking any laws?"

"As long as they're on resort property and the resort hasn't stated it's against the rules, there's not much we can do. That's something you'll have to bring up with your boss. Let's go back to when you found the body. You said Willow led you to the body?"

"Cats are a lot smarter than people give them credit for. I think she must have smelled something and you know how animals are. They can sense things like death. I think she knew what I was doing there and helped."

"What time did you hear the screams?"

I thought back to what Oscar said when he delivered the rat around three in the morning. It would have been a little before then, I guessed.

"Around three?"

"Why were you up at three?"

"I heard meowing outside my cabin. Luna's mate, Oscar, was outside. I guessed he must have been able to follow her scent or something."

"Did you notice anyone else who had a problem with Mark? Staff or a guest?"

He kept shifting the direction of his questions, and I had a feeling he was trying to catch me off guard. I rolled with the punches.

"No one was as overt about their dislike as Edgar, but the overall feeling was that he wasn't well liked among the competitors. As for the staff, I can't say that anyone disliked him. In fact, other than..."

I trailed off as I remembered what Penny said about Mark the day before and my face felt hot.

"Other than?"

I felt steeped in misery as I answered.

"Penny. She said something to the effect that a man like him should be put down. I got the impression that there may have been history between the two of them, but I don't know for sure."

Ethan met my eyes again, and I winced. I'd already suspected Penny of murder once, and here I was, doing it again. If she ever found out I was the one who said something, she'd never let me live it down. Provided, of course, she was innocent.

"I'll check into it."

"Oh, please don't let her know I said anything. She already hates my guts. This will only make it worse."

"I'll keep your name out of it. Anything else you noticed? You're very observant. I've noticed people confide in you. You make them feel safe with your warmth."

I flushed again at his compliment.

"Well, there is one thing, but I don't know how important it is. I found the body first, and then Trevor joined me. Once Dave found us, he trampled over all the prints that were leading to the body, even though we shouted at him to stop. I'm not sure if it means anything, but I thought that was odd. If he hadn't done that, you might have been able to match up prints or something."

Ethan leaned back and rubbed his forehead.

"It doesn't help, but there's not much we can do with footprints. It's not quite like it is in the movies. Anything else?"

"Not right now. I'll think about it, though. I've told you everything."

His eyes shuttered and a little thorn pricked my heart. I hadn't told him absolutely everything, but I'd done the best I could without revealing my secret.

"Okay. If you could send Trevor and Josh in next, that would be great. We'll need to get the guests rounded up. Can you also let an officer know to get them ready?"

"Sure."

I sat for a moment more, feeling unsettled, but brushed it off and left my office, feeling as though a weight was still sitting on my shoulders. I motioned Trevor over and passed along Ethan's message before finding an officer and doing the same thing. Charlie and Wendy watched me from the desk, eyes wide.

Charlie grabbed my arm and pulled me to the side.

"What happened? What did he ask you?"

I glanced over at the knot of uniformed police and shushed her.

"Not so loud. It was just the usual questions. I think he's going to go through all the staff before he starts on the guests."

"Well, I slept through everything," Wendy put in, shaking her head. "I can't believe it. Who do you think did it?"

A guilty flash of what I'd told Ethan about Penny flitted through my mind, but I shrugged.

"It's hard to say."

Charlie watched me, eyes narrowed, but thankfully, she let it go. She'd get it out of me later, without a doubt.

"Do you think he'll want to talk to me?" Charlie asked.

"I think all of us are on the list. Do you remember anything about the snowmobiles last night?"

Charlie popped her gum and frowned.

"I think one had reddish trim, but I'm uncertain. Why?"

"Ethan asked me about it. I wonder who was driving them?"

"Hard to say. I suppose we could go outside and see if any of them look familiar."

I turned to Wendy, excitement leaping within.

"Do you mind manning the desk alone? We'll be right back."

I pulled Charlie through the door while she squawked about our coats.

"We'll freeze to death out here, Eden! What's the hurry?"

"I just had an idea, and I wanted to see if Mark's sled was the one we saw. I'm still trying to figure out why he was out there on foot. Do you remember if there were more people on those sleds last night?"

"It happened so fast," Charlie said, slowing down. "But I think it was just two."

"Well, maybe they came back for the sled with another person. Let's go see if we can peek in the trailers. Some of them are open. I know Dave mentioned that Mark's sled was outside. Wait..."

I stopped right in the middle of the parking lot as a thought smacked me in the face.

"Charlie, when Dave walked up to the desk this morning, did he come from the elevator or outside? I wasn't paying attention."

"The elevator. I think. I'm pretty sure."

"Then how did he know Mark's sled was right outside? He's the one who trampled through the footprints leading to the body. What if was an act, and he knew where Mark was all along?"

Charlie brightened and grabbed my arm.

"You're right. No one went outside in the hour before you showed up. It was just me. I would've seen someone walk past. Which trailer is Mark's?"

I looked around the lot and realized I didn't know. My shoulders sank.

"I don't know. They all look alike. I guess we could check the plates. Do you know where he's from?"

"He's a local. Greenville I think."

"Greenville? That's weird. That's the second time I've heard of that town today. Amber is from there."

"Hmmm. Well, this one's open. Let's check the truck plate and see if we can tell where it's from."

She pulled me towards the attached pickup and gave a sharp cry of victory.

"This has to be his. That's a Weldon County plate. Let's look in the trailer."

We retraced our steps and peeked inside. Two sleds were parked beneath the low slung roof, and the closest one had red trim. Charlie squealed.

"I'd have to look at them all, but I'm pretty sure this was the sled I saw last night."

"We've got to let Ethan know," I said, turning towards the lodge. "We might have just cracked this case wide open."

We hurried back as the wind whipped through the parking lot, chilling me to the bone. Charlie was right. We should've taken our coats. But within minutes, we were back inside and I stood for a second in the entryway as the heater blew right in my face.

"Eden, what do I say to him? Can you come back there with me? I'm scared."

"It's Ethan, Charlie. He's not scary. But, yes, I can go with you if you think it will help."

We went back towards my office and stopped in the hallway when I realized the door was closed.

"Who's in there?"

"Probably Trevor and Josh."

"Can you hear anything?"

"I don't think so, but I can try."

I stepped closer to the door and put my ear against it. All I could pick up was a low hum of voices, but there was no way of telling who was speaking. I was just about to step back when the door popped open, revealing a sour faced Penny. Her eyes narrowed in rage.

"Detective Rhodes, this busy-body was just listening to our conversation," she said, grabbing my arm and yanking me inside. "I thought this was a confidential meeting."

I felt like a kid busted for snooping.

"I heard nothing. We just got here. Ethan, Charlie's got something that I think may help. She's right out there."

"That will be all, Miss Langston. For now."

Penny's eyes held a threat of retribution as she gave me one more long look before hustling past. Ethan's lips turned up at the corner as he watched me.

"You always step in it, don't you? Now, what's this about Charlie?"

Charlie popped her head inside and cracked her gum.

"Whew, I don't think she saw me. Now, let's get down to the brass tacks. Ethan, I think we've got a huge lead for you."

She settled into the chair across from Ethan and unleashed a triumphant grin. I leaned against the wall, hoping that we'd found something that would indeed crack the case.

Chapter Ten

F ive short minutes later, I left my office with my bubble completely burst. Ethan thanked us for what we considered a bombshell, and promised to look into it, without seeming that interested. After that, he'd asked me to leave so he could get Charlie's statement, and so here I was, wandering back to the front desk, wondering what in the heck I was going to do with the rest of my day.

Working in my office was out of the question, and to be perfectly honest, marketing and public relations were the farthest thing from my mind. Technically, it was Spring Break, even though I was an online student, and I didn't even have my courses to keep me busy. I joined Wendy and let out a piteous sigh that caught her attention.

"Eden? What's wrong? Have they found the killer?"

"No. Charlie and I thought we had a great lead, but Ethan doesn't seem that interested. Is there anything you need help with? I don't know what to do with myself."

Wendy shrugged and pulled her sweater sleeves down over her wrists.

"Not really. I have little to do. Josh and Trevor already herded everyone into the ballroom, and the kitchen staff is watching everyone with them. Penny and her team are cleaning the rooms while everyone's out of them, and I'm just sitting here twiddling my thumbs. Danny's outside helping Carl with the shoveling and snow removal, and it's too cold for me to want to pitch in and help with that."

I let out another sigh and drummed my fingers on the desk. The sound of popping gum caught my attention and Charlie came out of the hallway.

"Whew. I know you said Ethan isn't scary, but he can be super intense. I felt like admitting to things I didn't even do. So, what do we do now?"

She bumped me with a hip as she stood next to me, and I couldn't help but marvel at her energy.

"I was just trying to figure that out. Aren't you exhausted? You were up all night."

"Nah, I'm wired. I may have had a few too many cups of coffee, too. So, here's what I'm thinking. Obviously, you can't get any work done in your office, and this place is quiet right now. So... let's solve the murder!"

Typically, I'd jump at the chance to dip my amateur toes into the investigative waters, but I was still smarting after Ethan's dismissal of our clue. I shrugged and stared down at my feet.

"It sounds like he's got it under control."

Charlie knocked her knuckles against my forehead.

"Um, hello? Where's my Eden and what have you done with her? Come on, just because he thought little of our clue doesn't mean that's the only one out there. We just need more evidence. Besides, don't you need to look in on the cats? You said the body was discovered right near where the clowder lives, so that sounds like a great place to start. I'll come with you, since taking care of the cats is a big job," she said, winking and nudging me with her elbow. "Besides, you have a reason to be in the forest and it's not like the cops can force you to stop taking care of the cats. And if we stumble on some clues that solve the case, so be it!"

I brightened, remembering Benny. He needed help, and

maybe with Charlie along, I could convince him to come with us. He seemed to like her, or at least the sound of her voice. I nodded.

"Let's do it. I need to trap Benny so we can get him to the vet. He liked you. Let's go see if we can get him."

Charlie shot me a thumb's up and shrugged into her coat before tossing me my gear.

"Wendy, just text if you need anything. We won't be too far away."

Wendy shuddered and looked out the window.

"You guys are braver than I am. Maybe later I can come by and see the kittens, Eden?"

I patted her arm.

"Of course. You'll love them. Let's go, Charlie."

She bounced outside ahead of me and I wondered just how many cups of coffee she'd had. Maybe I needed to drink more of the stuff. We stopped at the cabin to grab Jasper's carrier and looked in on the snoozing cats. Charlie's squeal of delight woke everyone, much to their displeasure, but Luna quickly softened and allowed my friend to have a look at the kittens.

I gave Jasper a quick kiss and whispered our plans to him before heading back outside. As we walked towards the forest, my stomach rumbled, and I'd wished I grabbed something to eat before we headed this way.

Charlie chattered throughout our walk, and we tossed around different theories on who might have wanted Mark dead. Edgar was still in the lead, but my instincts kept shouting that he was the wrong suspect, as much as I wanted it to be right. The older man was incredibly unlikeable, and had made a huge scene, threatening Mark. But it just didn't add up. At least not yet.

We got to the clearing and waited, hoping the cat would pop up. It wasn't the usual time I came by, but within a few minutes, I heard a familiar raspy meow and turned to see Fig looking at me, curiosity blazing out of her intelligent yellow eyes.

"Hi, Fig," I said, glancing at my friend. "I'm sorry about all the upheaval."

Charlie crouched down and reached a hand towards the brown cat, who quickly backed away.

"She's so beautiful. Look at that coat. It looks like a mink."

I wasn't sure Fig appreciated being compared to a rodent, but the first part of Charlie's compliment obviously pleased her. I needed to pass along my request to Fig without Charlie realizing I was actually talking to her. I looked at Fig, and then at the bag, and then turned to Charlie.

"Hopefully we'll be able to find Benny. He sounded terrible this morning. I'm worried about him."

Fig's eyes narrowed, and she melted away into the trees. I stood, indecisive about whether I should follow her, but waited.

"You said they all live in dens around here?"

"Yep, it's really cool how organized they are. Cats are amazing creatures."

"I know. I miss mine. He was always so cool. Hey, what's that?"

Rustling noises came through the trees and I spotted Benny being herded forward by Fig, whose ears were laid back flat to her head. She stayed a safe distance away, but from what I could pick up from her conversation, she was demanding he go with us in no uncertain terms.

Benny looked listless as he sat in front of us, eyes down. His breathing was so loud it made my heart hurt. I glanced at Fig and she gave me a sharp nod. I could only hope his obedience to Fig would stretch towards getting into a kennel without scratching one of us.

"Oh, sweet boy," Charlie said, holding out a hand towards him. "Come on, buddy. We won't hurt you."

I zipped open the bag and knelt next to it, hoping he'd take the hint. With a cough, Benny stood and slowly walked into it, hissing at me as he curled into the bag. I closed my eyes and zipped it up as fast as I could. Whew. We'd captured him.

"Let's take him to the vet. I'll have to come back later with some food for the other cats. It's going to be hard for them to hunt with all these people in the woods making a bunch of noise."

Fig's eye roll told me she got the message loud and clear, and it was completely unnecessary to state the obvious, but Charlie didn't know that. She nodded and stood. I reached down to pick up the bag, while Benny hissed and spat. I stepped back and Charlie shook her head.

"Now, Benny. That's not nice. I'll carry you."

Whatever it was about Charlie, Benny obviously trusted her. He remained quiet, his labored breathing the only sound he made, as we walked back to the resort.

"We can take my car," I said. "Hopefully, the vet can look at him right away."

"I'll call them while you drive."

Ethan was standing outside talking to a uniformed officer as we walked through the parking lot. He started jogging towards us as Charlie loaded Benny into the car.

"What's up?"

"We finally caught that sick cat from the clowder. We're taking him to the vet. It's okay if we leave, right?"

Ethan poked his head into the backseat and jumped as Benny hissed.

"Yeah, sure. I've already got your statements. Is he alright?"

I closed the door and glanced at Charlie before turning to Ethan.

"I don't know, but I hope so. He sounds so congested. I'm really worried about him. He's not the friendliest cat, but he needs help."

Ethan's eyes softened as he tilted his head to the side, looking at me.

"You're something else, Eden. I meant to tell you earlier to be careful out there. Until we find out who killed Chesney, you could be at risk. Especially since you spend so much time in the woods."

I nodded and put my hand on the top of my door.

"Will do. We should be back later. If there's anything we can do to help with the investigation, let me know."

And just like that, the friendly look in his eyes went cold. He stepped back and shook his head.

"Just let me do my job. I know you've been very lucky with finding clues, but leave this one to me, okay?"

He rapped on the top of my car and walked off. I grumbled as I slid into the car, bonking my head as I did.

"Ow. Dang it."

"Oh, Eden. When will the two of you ever figure out that you're perfect for each other? He really cares for you."

"Well, I don't know if the feeling is mutual right now. He basically told me to butt out of his investigation."

"Yeah, like that's going to happen. Anyway, the vet's got a spot for us, but we need to hurry."

I was more than happy to focus on driving instead of thinking about Ethan and the murder. I checked Benny in the rearview mirror and the poor tuxedo cat looked miserable. It was probably his first time in a vehicle, and he didn't look like he was a fan of this type of transport.

Once we were at the vet, Charlie jumped out and grabbed his bag, with nary a hiss to be heard. I held open the door for her as the receptionist peered over the desk.

"Is this our wild cat?"

"Yes. Thanks for getting us in on such short notice."

"Not a problem. If you'll both follow me back, we'll get him ready for the vet. She'll be here shortly. She's just wrapping up another examination."

She led us back into the same room where I'd waited with Jasper when he'd been ill. The vet tech put a hand on the bag, which made Benny hiss and yowl. She backed away while Charlie crooned to the cat.

"He seems to like me. Maybe I can get him out of there."

The tech nodded while checking to ensure the two entrances into the room were tightly sealed.

"If he doesn't want to be touched, we'll have to sedate him. Please be careful that he doesn't bite you."

Charlie reached in without a care and lifted the skinny cat out of the bag like she'd owned him her whole life. He lay in her arms, not purring, but at least not hissing or fighting. She stroked his head, and he relaxed.

"Amazing. It looks like you're his person," she said, smiling at Charlie.

"We just met, but I think you're right."

The back door to the room opened and the same vet I'd seen before walked in. Benny didn't even move as she began her examination, brows furrowed.

"He's in awful shape. Is this another one of the resort cats?"

"Yes. He appeared a week ago, I think. If it hadn't been for Charlie, I don't think I would've caught him. Is there anything you can do for him?"

"I'll treat him with some antibiotics, but I need to run some blood tests. He might have FIV or FELV. He'll need to be kept inside, isolated from other cats until I can get the results back. Can you do that?"

I tried to think of what to do, but Charlie nodded.

"He can stay with me. I'll look after him."

"Great. I'll treat him for fleas and send you with some medication you can give him for the cough and his congestion. He doesn't seem that old. I'd say he was about four or five."

Benny meowed weakly as she drew blood, but he didn't struggle. Charlie held him close and murmured to him, keeping him calm. He barely moved as the vet put two pills down his throat and instructed Charlie on what she needed to do. My friend carefully tucked Benny back into the carrier once the vet was done.

"I'm glad you could bring him in. Another day out in this weather and I don't think he would've made it. As it is, it's going to be touch and go. Girls, I hate to say this, but it's probably a good idea not to get attached."

Charlie's eyes were misty as she patted the carrier.

"Too late, doc. I know what you're saying, though. I'll do my best to take care of him."

"How's your old boy holding up, Eden?"

"Great," I said. "He's happy and running around like a kitten. Speaking of, Luna had kittens. I've got them in my cabin. I should book an appointment to get their vaccinations."

"Kittens in this weather? It's a good thing you have a place for them. We'll get you booked in. Anything else?"

"I think that's it," Charlie said, picking up the bag. "What do I owe you?"

"I'll ring you up out front," the tech said, opening the door for us. "We'll need to get your contact information for the blood test results, or do you just want us to call Eden?"

"You can call me," Charlie said, rattling off her number as she grabbed for her wallet.

I put a hand on her arm to stop her.

"I can pay for it."

"Nope, I've got this. Benny's mine and I'm going to take care of him."

She got her owner's record updated and paid the bill. We'd need to stop and grab some cat supplies while we were in town. I had a feeling that Benny had a good chance of surviving, especially with Charlie's sheer force of will in play. We walked back to the car and headed for the pet shop while Charlie gazed at Benny, who was sleeping soundly.

"I hope he's going to be okay. He reminds me so much of my cat. Do you think that's possible, Eden? For cats to come back into your life?"

"You know, I think anything is possible and things happen for a reason," I said, as I parked near the front of the shop. "I'll run in and grab a few things for you if you want to keep him company."

"Get him a few toys. I wonder if he's ever played before?"

I left the two of them and quickly rounded up everything she'd need for the first few days of Benny's convalescence. By the time I got back to the car, Charlie and Benny were both asleep. I loaded the purchases as quietly as I could and turned down the radio as I started the car.

Charlie stirred, but quickly fell back asleep as I pulled onto the highway. The roads were nicely plowed, but the wind had picked up, leaving the roads icy as snow blew across them. I slowed down and paid attention to the road, hoping my old car and its not great tires would make it back okay.

A horn startled me as a huge pickup roared up behind me, its grill huge in my rearview mirror. It honked again, waking Charlie, who looked around with bleary eyes before shouting.

"Eden! He's going to hit us!"

I white-knuckled the steering wheel, refusing to speed up, but easing over to the side of the road to let them pass. The horn blared again, and the engine revved as we came up to a blind turn. I was shaking as I slowed further, praying they'd do the same.

I couldn't see into the pickup cab as I risked a glance over my shoulder. My little car jolted as the pickup rammed into it. Benny's yowl, coupled with Charlie's shriek, nearly made me scream myself.

Once we were past the turn, the pickup pulled up next to us, and I realized the windows were tinted so dark, there was no way of seeing in. The pickup stayed right next to us, matching my speed.

"What in the actual hell is he doing? He's going to get us killed!" Charlie squealed.

The window of the pickup rolled down and the barrel of a gun appeared, making my blood run cold. This couldn't be happening.

Chapter Eleven

Another car appeared on the horizon, in the lane the pickup was in now. My hands were shaking as I hit the brakes, skidding to a stop on the shoulder of the road. Charlie grabbed my arm, screaming.

"What are you doing? We're sitting ducks!"

"Get the plate number! If they don't get over, they're going to crash into that car."

The pickup swerved back into our lane and took off, slipping and sliding on the icy road as its back end fishtailed. The other driver laid on the horn before rolling down their window and giving the pickup a gesture.

They slowed as they got to us and I saw a man in the driver's seat who looked familiar.

"Are you girls okay? What was wrong with that man?"

"I don't know," I said, hands shaking so hard I had to grip the steering wheel again. "He just came up on us. Charlie, did you get the plate?"

She grabbed her phone and nodded.

"I've gotta write it down before I forget. It wasn't a local plate.

We've got to report this. Do you mind letting the police know what you saw?"

"Absolutely. You girls work out at the resort, don't you? I'm a cashier at the grocery store."

That's why he looked familiar. I relaxed a little and tried to smile.

"We do. Thank you for stopping. He hit the back of my car. I need to check for damage."

"Let me turn around up there and I can help you look. I have a little experience with cars. Oh, I'm Jeremy."

"I'm Eden and this is Charlie."

He rolled up his window and drove forward. Charlie had already called the police department and was giving our location as I turned back to her. I turned off the engine and made sure my hazards were on. There wasn't a lot of traffic on this road, but the last thing I needed was for someone to ram into my car again. Charlie took the phone away from her ear for a second.

"Was the pickup black or blue? I'm terrible with dark colors."

"Black with tinted windows. Was that really a gun or was I imagining it?"

"It was a gun. It looked like one of my dad's rifles. I can't believe it," she said, putting the phone back to her ear and relaying the color to the dispatcher. "We'll sit tight, thank you."

Jeremy pulled in behind us and I got out, slipping a little on the pavement as I walked to the back of my car. My tail light was broken and a largish dent covered half of the back of my car.

"Are the police coming?"

"Yep," Charlie shouted out the window. "They're sending someone from the resort. I guess everyone's over there. It shouldn't take long."

He nodded and let out a whistle as he saw the damage on the car.

"I hope you've got insurance. At least no one was injured. What on earth possessed someone to do this? Was it road rage?"

"I don't know. I was just driving along and they appeared behind me. I've never seen that pickup before in my life."

The passenger door opened and Charlie joined us.

"Son of a biscuit, that's a lot of damage," she said, frowning. "Did you cut them off or something?"

"No, they came out of nowhere."

"Well, I'll stick around until the cops get here, but I need to call my work and let them know I'll be late."

Charlie smiled at him, and Jeremy's face flushed as he walked back to his car.

"He's nice. And cute."

I thought about Danny back at the resort, but held my tongue. He still apparently hadn't decided if he wanted to be more than friends with Charlie, and I knew he valued their friendship. I was going to let them figure it out. As Jeremy joined us, a patrol car passed us before whipping around and pulling in behind. A familiar person was sitting in the passenger seat.

"Eden! Are you okay? Do we need to call the paramedics?"

Ethan rushed over, his face drawn with worry, but I shook my head.

"No, we're fine. That's more than I can say for my poor car, though."

"What happened?"

I took a deep breath before describing the pickup and how they'd rammed my car. Jeremy gave his statement to the officer while we talked with Ethan. He frowned and looked back towards town.

"You didn't see them following you?"

"No. I was worried about the road conditions. My tires aren't great, and it was getting really slick. I didn't notice them until I heard their horn."

"How about you, Charlie?"

"I was sound asleep until the horn woke me. The gun scared me. If it hadn't been for Jeremy passing by, who knows what they would've done?"

"Gun?"

"Didn't dispatch tell you?" Charlie asked, flushing. "I told them it was a rifle."

Ethan cursed softly under his breath and glanced towards the officer, who was still talking to Jeremy.

"Shaun left that part out. He just said it was two girls from the resort who'd been involved in a road rage incident. I knew you were gone, so I rode along. Dear God, Eden, you could've been killed."

I rubbed my arms, shivering as the adrenaline spike wore off.

"Have you run the plates yet?"

"It came back as stolen from Nebraska. You didn't see the driver?"

"No, the windows were so tinted I couldn't see in when they pulled up next to us. When he was behind me, he was so close I couldn't see into the cab."

He rubbed his forehead and held up a hand before walking over to join the officer and Jeremy. They were too far away for me to hear what they were saying, but I found myself not caring. I just wanted to go home and curl up in bed with Jasper.

"Is Benny okay? I'm sure this excitement has terrified him."

Charlie peeked into the backseat and smiled.

"He's out cold. Poor little guy. He's had quite the day. I need to get him back to my cabin."

"Do you think the car will be okay to drive back to the resort? I don't feel like hanging around in town all day."

Ethan rejoined us and broke in.

"It will be fine to wait. I don't want you running around town alone, anyway. Have you called your insurance company yet?"

"No, not yet."

"I'll get the police report number and text it to you for them. Shaun's going to take a few pictures and you'll be free to go. We'll follow you back to the resort."

My hands were still shaking as I pulled back onto the road and headed back home. My car seemed to be fine, but I wasn't in any hurry to push it. Charlie and I sat in silence, broken only by the sound of Benny's breathing. Was I imagining it, or did he already sound better?

A rush of relief filled my soul as I turned onto the resort road. Even though a murder had taken place, it still felt like an oasis of calm compared to what we'd experienced on the road. I parked as close to the cabins as I could since we had a bunch of stuff to carry.

"Oh shoot. I didn't even think about the stuff in the trunk. I hope nothing was broken when we got rammed."

I hopped out and rushed to the back, struggling to lift the trunk's lid.

"Here, let me help," Ethan said, appearing next to me. "It's bent from the impact. It drove okay, though?"

"Just fine. Hopefully, my insurance will cover all the damages. I have a little put aside, but not enough for expensive repairs."

"Go to the shop in town and let them know I sent you. They'll give you a fair price."

"I used them when I first got here and they were nice. Great idea."

With a mighty pull, Ethan got the trunk open, even though it let out a shriek of twisted metal as it rose. I dug through the bags, relieved to see nothing was broken.

"Whew. All of Benny's things are okay."

Ethan huffed out a laugh and shook his head.

"You always worry about everyone else, but not yourself. Why is that?"

"Eldest daughter syndrome?" asked Charlie as she lifted Benny's bag out of the backseat. "That's what I think, anyway."

I shrugged and felt my face flush.

"Maybe. I never really thought of that before. I only had one sister, though, so it's not like I was raising a ton of siblings."

Ethan reached for the bags in the trunk at the same time I did and our hands brushed. He shot me a smile and chose the heaviest bag.

"I'll help you get this to Charlie's cabin, and then I need to get back to questioning the guests. I put in a request to keep everyone off their snowmobiles until our techs go through them all for evidence. It will buy your cat friends a little quiet, at least for a day or two. It's going to take some time to question everyone."

Astonished by his thoughtfulness, I searched for the right thing to say as I attempted to close the trunk lid. He reached up and slammed it down.

"Thank you, Ethan. That was very thoughtful."

His neck flushed, and he dipped his head before looking at Charlie.

"Lead the way and we'll follow. I know Eden's in Cabin Ten, but I can't remember which one is yours."

"Eight," Charlie said, popping her gum. "The place is a wreck, but hopefully Benny won't mind. I'll have to be tidier now that I have a roommate."

She opened the door to her cabin, and I realized she wasn't kidding. Clothes were strewn all over the place, and her face flamed nearly as red as the underside of her hair as she tossed a bra behind a chair.

"I'll help you get Benny settled," I said before turning towards Ethan. "I'll be up at the lodge in a few minutes. I'm sure Wendy needs a break."

He nodded, and his eyes shuttered a little, blocking out the emotions that had been streaming out just moments before. He waved at Charlie and headed back outside, closing the door behind him.

"You didn't need to get rid of him that fast," Charlie said, clucking as she unzipped Benny's bag. "He was enjoying being around you."

I busied myself emptying the bags and ignored her statement. I'd been enjoying his company, too, but I still felt awkward around Ethan.

"I've got the same brand of food Jasper likes, but I don't know if Benny will enjoy it. If not, we can try something else."

Charlie took the food from my hand and rolled her eyes.

"Fine. Don't talk about it. Where should I put the litter box?"

"Normally I'd say out of the way, but until Benny's feeling better, I'd keep it nearby. Speaking of him, where did he go?"

There were about five hundred different places he could hide in the chaos of Charlie's room, but I spotted him curled up on her bed, next to her pillow. I couldn't help but smile at how sweet he looked when he was asleep and not hissing at me.

"You're sure you'll be okay with him?"

"Absolutely," Charlie said. "And if not, my best friend is a wonder with cats. I swear, sometimes you can actually talk with them the way you communicate."

She looked at me and I flushed and looked away. She was kidding, right? I sure hoped so. When I first learned about my ability to talk to cats, I hadn't thought about the fact that it meant I'd need to lie to my best friend. And to a man I cared about. A lot. I decided I was being over reactive and let her comment slide.

"Get some rest. See you at dinner? Or do you want me to bring some by so you can get some extra sleep?"

"Nah, I'll be there. If I don't stay on my schedule, I'll be a wreck. Do you think the cops are going to be here all night?"

"I'm uncertain, but I'm still going to feed the cats tonight. I can't miss it, not with it being so cold out. See you later, Charlie."

She answered by letting out an enormous yawn, and I laughed as I closed the door. I turned to walk towards the resort when the overwhelming feeling of being watched crept over me, making my skin crawl. I stopped and looked around, but everything was quiet. That was odd. I kept going, putting it down to just too many nerves.

Chapter Twelve

A tickling sensation on my cheek gently pulled me towards awareness the next morning and I smiled as I opened my eyes to see Jasper's golden gaze trained on my face. His whiskers quirked, tickling me again.

"Good morning, Jasper. Did you sleep well?"

He purred and snuggled into my neck with his chilly nose. Mornings like these made everything worthwhile.

"I did. The young uns did as well, but I can hear them moving around. I figured I'd wake you before they did. You slept soundly."

I nodded, surprised. I had slept well, particularly considering the day I'd had yesterday. Once the excitement had died down, the rest of my day had been almost normal. I'd kept out of Ethan's investigation and had busied myself helping Wendy before coming back to my cabin to read and spend time with the cats. I rolled over, carefully avoiding Jasper, and looked over at Luna's makeshift den.

"I should get the playpen set up. They sound like they're getting more active."

I eased out of bed while Jasper immediately moved into the warm spot I'd left behind. Oh cats. I tiptoed over to Luna and watched as the kittens clumsily crawled around, mewing quietly.

"Good morning, Luna."

She blinked her eyes and stretched, yawning widely.

"Did Oscar come last night? Once these little ones quieted down, I slept hard. I didn't hear him."

I straightened and shook my head, glancing towards the door. If he had come, I hadn't heard him either. I walked over and cracked open the door, but there were no gifts for Luna on the step.

"No, he must not have stopped by."

"I hope he's okay. Did you see him last night when you brought the clowder's food?"

"I thought I did, but it was dark by the time I got there and you know how hard he is to see at night. I'll check on everyone this morning and make sure he's okay."

Luna nodded and nosed one of the exploring kittens towards her stomach. Their coats were coming in, but it was still hard to tell what color they were going to be. I poured out food for everyone, making sure Luna had extra, before making my own quick breakfast.

Okay, making was a strong word for opening a carton of yogurt and popping a piece of toast in the toaster, but it was tasty. At least I wouldn't get waylaid from eating since I ate at home. After the past two days, I cherished the chance to eat my breakfast in peace.

Once I'd finished, I tackled my playpen project while Jasper watched with interest from the bed, supervising my progress.

"I think that part goes on that side," he said while I tried to get the last parts to come together.

I followed his instructions and breathed a sigh of relief as it fit perfectly.

"There you go, Luna. We can put your bed inside and I'll line the bottom with a blanket to make it soft for the babies."

I winced as I realized that meant taking a blanket off the bed. I'd forgotten to buy one during our trip to town the day before. I'd have to remember to replace it, or at least wash it very well.

Once everyone was settled, Luna nodded her approval before bending down to bathe each kitten thoroughly. I sat on the floor and watched, marveling at how quickly they were growing.

"What's the plan for today?" Jasper asked as he jumped down and sharpened his claws on the rug.

"It all depends on if Ethan finished interviewing the guests and I can use my office again. If he hasn't, I'll have to keep myself busy. I suppose I could ask Mr. Marsburg if I could borrow his office. I feel guilty that I'm not getting much work done."

"You're not investigating on your own?"

I wrapped my arms around my knees and shrugged.

"I don't know," I said, looking down. "Ethan made it pretty clear he doesn't want any help. I can't even be mad at him because he's making sure the snowmobilers won't go tearing around the forest, bothering the cats."

"Hmmm."

I glanced at Jasper as he tucked into his food, his face turned from mine. He didn't need to say it. I never passed up an opportunity to investigate, so why was I so hesitant this time around? Was I going soft? Did the incident with the pickup scare me that much? I sure didn't like the feeling that was swimming around in my stomach.

I got up, made the bed and got ready to face the day, firmly pushing my thoughts, doubts and suspicions down. Ethan was a trained investigator, and I was... not. It was his job, not mine. I had enough to do without sticking my nose where it didn't belong. Right? I sighed, frustrated with myself, and finished tidying up my cabin.

"I'll see how Benny's doing," I said as I put on my coat. "Charlie should still be at the front desk. Maybe he saw something and I can pass that information on to Ethan somehow."

Jasper nodded, but his golden eyes never left my face. He enjoyed sleuthing as much as I did, and I felt like I was letting him down. I turned away and walked through the door, locking it behind me. Ugh. I didn't like this feeling at all.

I trudged through the snow with my hands shoved into my pockets, watching as my boots kicked up little puffs of snow. Would Spring ever truly come? Maybe that's what was wrong with me. I grew up in the southern part of the state, where winter had already fled, and I wasn't used to the mountains.

I pushed through the doors in time to see Charlie pop her head up from behind the desk. She relaxed when she saw me and bent back down as I joined her, curious. I shrugged out of my coat and smiled as I saw why she was acting so strangely.

"Hi Benny. Feeling better, bud?"

He didn't hiss, which was progress, but his greenish eyes never left my face as I stood back up. His breathing wasn't audible, and he looked much better, cuddled up in his little bed on the shelf below the computer.

"I couldn't leave him alone all night in my cabin," Charlie said. "I don't think the boss would mind, but I'm keeping an eye out for Penny. She'd raise holy heck if she saw him."

I glanced around again, worried. All we needed was for her to show up.

"I can cover for you if you want to take him back to your cabin. Her shift is starting any minute. Was it a pretty quiet night?"

"Thanks, Eden! Yeah, hardly anyone came down. That Dave guy hung out in the lounge by himself for a little while, but everyone else kept to their rooms. The kitchen staff was busy handling room service. I hope they all get some bonuses," she said as she put on her coat, zipping it halfway.

"No kidding. You'd better hurry. Did you bring his carrier?"

"I just carried him. He's the sweetest little cat. I hope I can keep him, even when he's better. We vibe."

I watched in amazement as she picked up the formerly surly cat and tucked him into her coat, zipping him in securely. She beamed as she peeked inside.

"Just a few minutes, buddy, and you'll be back in your cabin. I'll come back and grab your stuff."

She hustled around the desk, never breaking stride as Penny walked in through the door, giving her an unfriendly glare. The head of housekeeping stopped and watched Charlie leave while I held my breath. She turned and gave me a malevolent look before saying something under her breath and hustling off, heels rapping loudly on the tile floor.

I relaxed once the sound carried far enough away. At least with Penny, you always knew where she was, thanks to the shoes she insisted on wearing. That made me think about my suspicions about her and Mark. Had he been killed by someone he knew and trusted? Would Penny have had the strength to get him out into the forest and arrange him on a snowbank?

Shaking my head to clear it, I focused on tidying up the front desk. I gathered up Benny's things and stowed them in the tote bag Charlie left under the counter. I remembered seeing him near Mark's body as I folded his bed to make it fit. Would he talk to me? He was better, but it was clear he still didn't like me. How could I have a conversation with him and not let Charlie know about my abilities?

I groaned and stood, thoroughly frustrated. I hated keeping secrets, particularly from the people I cared about, and it was eating me alive. Was the secret of Mark's death also eating the killer alive?

The elevators pinged and my shoulders slumped as I spotted Edgar walking into the lobby. He was literally the last person I wanted to see, especially since I was alone at the desk. He was by himself and glanced over at me before looking out the window, standing with his back towards me.

Even though the desk was now clear, I tried to find something to keep me occupied as he continued to stand there, hands folded behind his back. Finally, he let out a loud sigh and turned towards me, his face flushed.

"Look, I know I'm not your favorite person, but could we talk?"

I blinked, startled, and nodded.

"Of course. Is everything okay with your room?"

"The room's fine. I've been a jerk, and I know it," he said, glancing around as he walked towards the desk. "The thing is, I've heard that you are known for investigating stuff and you've already solved two murders. I need your help."

My mouth fell open as I stood there, looking at Edgar. He looked incredibly uncomfortable as he shoved his hands into his pockets and looked at the floor. I asked the first question that popped into my mind.

"Where on earth did you hear that?"

"What? Oh. I heard a few of the housekeeper girls talking in the hall yesterday while they were cleaning rooms. It looks bad for me, and I need help. That cop is coming to interview me again this morning, and I know he thinks I did it. Heck, everyone heard my blowup with Mark before he went and got killed. Everyone thinks I did it."

"But you didn't?"

I watched his face, wishing that people came with a little neon sign over their heads proclaiming whether they were telling the truth.

"No. I swear to you, I'm innocent. I didn't like Mark. Hell, I hated the man. And I know for a fact he was a cheater. But I didn't kill him. Oh, I know what I said. But I didn't mean it. We all say things like that when we're upset. You've gotta help me. The actual killer is still out there. What if I'm next?"

I suppressed a snort as I looked at him. Was he telling me the truth? His bloodshot eyes were full of pleading as he looked at me. It must have taken a lot for him to come here, knowing that he'd treated all the hotel staff like dirt.

"But the cops, especially Detective Rhodes, are talented investigators. They'll find the right person."

"Don't you see, girl? They're against me. No one else got called in for a second interview. I've asked around. They want to close this case up and I'm the best suspect. I'm innocent!"

Edgar began pacing as he talked, and his florid face got even redder as he threw his arms around wildly. Was he innocent? Was this just a game to throw the police off his scent? There was only one way to find out. As much as I'd sworn I'd steer clear of this one, I couldn't. I just couldn't. I had to know the truth, and Edgar had inside knowledge that might point me towards the true killer. I took a deep breath and jumped.

"Okay, Mr. Hanson. I'll help. I don't know how much I can do, but I'll do my best. I'm going to need to ask you some questions, and I want you to be completely honest with me."

"Anything. I'll do whatever you want, tell you whatever you want."

His coloring faded a little as he calmed down, and I couldn't suppress the worried feeling that I was making a huge mistake by trusting this man. He acted like an overgrown toddler at the best of times. What was I getting myself into?

"Okay, let's get started. Where did you go after your fight with Mark in front of the dining hall?"

"Not here," Edgar said, looking around. "Can't we go somewhere else and talk privately? I don't want everyone to know."

A thread of fear wove its way down my spine as I remembered his threat to me the day before. Was he simply trying to get me to follow him so he could do away with me?

The doors slid open and my boss walked in, his hair tousled from the wind. He smiled, his handsome face creasing when he spotted me.

"Good morning, Eden. I didn't expect to see you behind the desk. Mr. Hanson, right? Nice to see you again."

Edgar shook Marsburg's hand, and I relaxed a fraction. Of course, he'd stayed here before, and was probably well known by all the other staff who'd worked here for years.

"Shame it has to be under these circumstances. I heard your girl here was good at investigating crimes and I was just asking her for help. The police think I'm the one who offed Chesney."

Marsburg tilted his head to the side and looked at me, eyes serious.

"That's a shame, but certainly they know you're a respected business owner. Of course, sometimes that doesn't matter, does it? I'll vouch for Eden. She's as smart as they come. If it wasn't for her, well, let's just say I'd be in a world of hurt. Eden, if you think there's a way we can help Mr. Hanson, you've got my permission to take time away from your duties. Where is everyone?"

Edgar nodded and turned towards me, eyes full of hope. I couldn't turn him down now, even if I'd wanted to.

"Charlie just ran to her cabin. She'll be right back," I said, glancing at my watch. "And Wendy will be in to relieve her in a few minutes. I need to ask Mr. Hanson some questions, but I didn't want to leave the desk and Ethan's been using my office. I don't know if it's okay to go in there."

"You can use mine and I'll watch the front," Marsburg said, cheerfully unwinding his scarf from around his neck. "It's been a long time since I've done this job. It will be good for me. When you're done, Mr. Hanson, I believe the catering staff will have breakfast ready."

I bit back a sigh and led Edgar down the hall and into Marsburg's office. The immense bay window looked out over the resort and Edgar stood in front of it while I got settled behind the desk. I waited until several moments of silence passed before repeating my earlier question.

"Where did you go after the fight with Mark?"

Edgar remained at the window, his hands on his hips, as he looked out over the grounds.

"This is a beautiful place. I'd forgotten that. We're always so focused on the competition, we stop looking at the beauty. It's a shame. I'll be the first to admit I get carried away. How old are you, girl?"

"Why does that matter?" I asked, irritated he'd avoided my question.

"You can't be thirty yet. When you get to my age, things change. Mark was just a few years younger than me, but it might have been decades for as well as he still rode. You slip when you get older. Your reaction time slows. Alcohol doesn't help," he said with a snort. "And I'm definitely guilty of using that as a crutch. I've known Mark for at least ten years. Raced against him several times. I knew he cheated, but I always thought I could beat him and do it honestly. Now, I'll never get that chance."

I blinked, surprised by the soft tone he was using. Gone was the blustering, irritating man who'd roared around the resort, demanding and posturing. In his place was an older man, grasping for the faded shreds of his youth. But I couldn't let that sway me or make me forget my questions.

"Where were you, Mr. Hanson?"

He turned towards me.

"I was in my room. Alone. Feeling like an old bull that should be put down. You saw what happened when we fought. I banged my knee pretty hard, and I just wanted to be alone and drink away the humiliation. It doesn't work like that, though. It never does."

"You're not limping," I said, remembering what I'd noticed the day before.

"I've got a brace on. It helps. And I don't want to show any weaknesses. These young pups are already better than I am. They don't need any encouragement to beat me. I don't have an alibi, but you've got to believe me. I didn't kill Mark. I've always had a terrible temper. High blood pressure, my doctor tells me. Maybe he's right. I didn't like Mark, but he didn't deserve to die that way. I need your help to figure out who killed him."

He sat heavily in the chair across from me and this time, he didn't hide his wince of pain as he reached for his knee. I could see the outline of the brace, so I knew he wasn't lying. At least about that. But what about everything else? Another question popped into my head and I let it out without thinking twice.

"Who do you think killed him?"

Edgar leaned forward, eyes gleaming.

"One of his team members. And I think I can prove it."

Thoughts of the way Dave had ruined the tracks leading to Mark's body reared their head in my mind as I sat on the edge of Marsburg's desk chair, waiting for Edgar to continue.

Chapter Thirteen

I studied Edgar's face while I wrestled with my patience, hoping to glean some clue from it. His eyes were bloodshot, his wrinkles deeply embedded. Now that he'd dropped his bombshell, he seemed content to wait. I restrained myself from sighing and waited, remembering something Hannah Murphy taught me. If you sit quietly, people are more likely to talk to fill the silence. I could only hope she was right.

"How much do you know about snowmobile racing?"

"Absolutely nothing," I said, relieved he'd finally cracked. "Why?"

"Well, it would help with background, but I'll nutshell it for you. We're a bunch of weekend warriors. Your typical competitor is blue collar, hardworking and they like to cut loose on the weekends and have some fun. Add in some friendly competition, brewskis, and some cute local women, and you've got yourself some fun."

"Okay, I can understand that. Mark seemed different, though."

Edgar made a finger gun sign and pointed it at me, and I couldn't help but remember yesterday's incident with the pickup. I shifted uneasily in Marsburg's office chair.

"I knew you were smart. He was different. He definitely wasn't one of us. He didn't have to work all week to scrape together the money to compete. Snowmobiles aren't cheap, and neither is traveling to the races. He was a trust fund baby, and he had plenty of money to burn."

I leaned back in my chair and frowned.

"Are you saying he was killed because he was rich?"

"No. But it probably didn't help. I'm getting to it," Edgar said, matching my frown with a pair of bushy eyebrows that met over his nose. "He could pay top dollar for his team. While the driver matters, it's usually your mechanics that win the races for you. My boys, now, they do it for the love of the sport and the free trips. His guys? They were bought and paid for. No loyalty beyond the bucks they were earning."

"Okay, but if he paid well, why would one of them kill him? Murdering the golden goose is a sure way to end up broke."

"Now you're getting me. What if you were about to lose that cushy job and you were angry about it? What then?"

"Mark was going to fire someone? How do you know?"

"Girlie, we know everything about everyone. Who had what for breakfast, and who spent a little too long on the pot? The only ones who know how to keep a secret are the mechanics. They're a closed mouth bunch. Usually. I told you I know Mark was a cheater. Now, how do you think I found that out?"

I leaned forward, creaking the chair a little.

"Because someone on his team told you."

He finger gunned again.

"You got it. Dave Shepherd showed up two days ago, after practice, and told me he had some interesting information that would help me win. It wasn't cheap, but it was worth it. He said the mechanic team has been supercharging the engines, giving Mark the edge."

"You paid him for this information? How much?"

Edgar shifted in his chair and a flush crept up his neck.

"Five hundred. But don't you see? It was worth it. I finally had proof that Mark was cheating. It was going to blow the circuit wide open. Do you know how much prize money Mark was raking in?"

"I still don't see how this ended up with Mark being killed by his teammate. Are you saying Dave is the killer?"

Edgar spread his hands wide and nodded.

"After our little mixup outside, I heard Dave got canned once Mark found out where I'd gotten that intel. He should have cleared out, but he's acting like he's still on the crew. Why? I think Dave didn't want to lose his job, and he lashed out, killed Mark, and he's trying to act like nothing ever happened."

"How do you know Dave was fired?"

Edgar shifted again and glanced out the window before mumbling something I couldn't hear.

"What was that?"

"I said I overheard them outside Mark's room. I went to his room to apologize for losing my head. I figured I had some solid evidence and I could convince Mark to drop out and save face. I was just about to knock when I heard raised voices inside. I put my ear up to the door, and that's when I heard Mark tell Dave he was done. I scurried back to my room before I got caught once I heard someone coming to the door. I heard one more thing, though. After Mark said he was fired and would never work in the sport again, Dave threatened him. He said 'watch your back. You won't see it coming.' Now, that's just as good as an admission of murder, if you ask me."

"Did you tell Detective Rhodes what you overheard?"

Edgar looked down at his hands.

"No. I didn't think he'd believe me. I'm suspect number one. I could have made all that up just to throw the cops off my scent."

"And did you?"

Edgar's bloodshot eyes met mine, and he shook his head.

"No, ma'am. I am telling you the truth."

"Well, you need to tell Ethan what you heard. If that's what happened, that gives Dave the most powerful motive for wanting to see Mark dead. You can't keep this to yourself."

"I haven't, have I? I've told you. Maybe you can pass that along? I heard you and the detective are pretty friendly."

Was this place just one big fount of gossip? I shook my head and stood.

"You'll still need to tell him yourself. Was there anything else?"

He grumbled and heaved himself upwards out of the chair, wincing again. Even though he was a big man, would he have had the strength to kill Mark? Was this little meeting all designed to throw the police off his scent? I didn't know, but a part of me thought Edgar's report rang true.

"No. I'll keep my ear to the ground, though. If I don't end up in the clink until the real killer is found. If you ask me, Dave is danger-ous. I have a bad feeling he'll strike again."

He lumbered out of the office, banging open the door, leaving me alone as I tried to process his warning. I stared out the window at the snowy forest and shook my head. This was a mess.

"Eden? Is everything okay?"

I turned and saw Ethan leaning against the door frame behind me. His sky-blue eyes were filled with concern as they met mine.

"I don't know. You need to talk to Edgar again. He didn't tell you everything."

He walked in and took a seat in the chair, stretching out his long legs.

"But he told you?"

"Yeah. I guess he heard I've got a knack for solving murders."

"Well, he's right. What did he say?"

I leaned against the desk and filled Ethan in, mentioning my concerns about Dave destroying the footprints again. He nodded before pinching the skin between his eyebrows.

"His alibi is weak, but the physical evidence doesn't seem to point to him. I'll have to pull him in and get a statement. Do you think he'll talk?"

"I think so. What physical evidence?"

Ethan's eyes crinkled up in the corners.

"I wish I could tell you, but I can't. You could help me with something, though, since you seem to cannot keep from inves-tigating."

I perked up, conveniently ignoring his wry tone.

"What?"

"One housekeeper is hiding something. I think Penny told her to keep her mouth shut. Maybe you can talk to her and convince her to come forward."

"Of course," I said, leaning forward as excitement quickened my pulse. "Who is it?"

"Alicia. She wanted to tell me something, but she clammed up and wouldn't budge. I'd appreciate it. You have a way about you."

There was an emotion in his eyes that made me drop mine and stare at the floor, even though I wanted to cheer. He was actually asking for my help! Alicia was a recent hire, brought on to replace Jemma, a former member of the staff who'd murdered a guest and tried to kill me.

"I'll do it. Are you going to be using my office again today?"

He stood and his shoulder brushed mine lightly as he walked towards the door.

"Just for a few hours. You'll be able to get back to work this afternoon. I appreciate the help. Let me know what you find out and leave the follow-up to me, okay? We still haven't found that pickup. Have you scheduled your car for repairs?"

"Not yet. I'll do that later today. I totally forgot about it with everything that's going on. Do you think it was the mechanic?"

"I don't know. I guess someone could have slipped past us. But that pickup wasn't in the lot. We checked. How's the cat doing?"

"Benny? I think he's going to pull through. Charlie and he are really hitting it off."

We stood there, awkwardly, for a moment before Ethan cleared his throat.

"Great. Talk to you later."

I checked my watch after he'd left. If I wanted to talk to one of Penny's girls, I was going to need to do it before their morning meeting. The last thing I needed was to irritate her any more than I already had. I hustled out of Marsburg's office and headed back to the front desk. Wendy was there, deep in conversation with our boss, so I kept going to the elevators, praying I'd make it down to the housekeeping room before Penny. I stepped inside and punched the door close button.

I'd spent little time in the basement, and I was surprised to see it was a hub of activity. The washers were going, making a racket so loud I could barely hear myself think. I popped my head into the breakroom and the three girls sitting there stood up, with matching harried looks on their faces. I recognized Amber and smiled.

"Good morning, Amber. How's the kitchen staff holding up?"

She glanced at Alicia and flared her eyes open before turning back to me with a smile that felt a little off and a lot fake.

"Just fine. I'll get back to work."

She brushed past me and hustled away before I had time to say anything else to her. I turned in time to see Alicia and the other girl exchange a look. What was going on here? I smiled at Alicia, hoping to break the ice.

"I'm Eden. I think we've met before."

"I remember you. You work with the suits upstairs. Is anything wrong?"

"No, not at all. I just wanted to talk. Do you have a minute?"

She and the other girl glanced at each other again, and I waited, swimming in awkwardness.

"Sure, but I've got a meeting in ten minutes. That old bag…"

Alicia trailed off, her face flushed bright red as the other girl made her escape with a muffled giggle.

"It's okay. Believe me, we all know what Penny's like."

Alicia relaxed and her color went back to normal, even though her eyes were still guarded. She kept glancing at the clock over the door, and I forged ahead before she bailed. She was more nervous than a cat, and I wasn't sure I was going to get anything out of her.

"How do you like it here? Are you settling in?"

She shrugged and looked down at the table.

"It's fine. It's a job. They're kind of hard to get these days, so I can't be too picky, even if Penny is a raging witch."

I sat next across from her and patted her hand before she snatched it away.

"I know it's hard. Has Penny, well, has she asked you to do

anything that has made you uncomfortable? I know it's difficult when we're all being interviewed by the police."

Alicia's sharp eyes met mine, and she shifted in her seat, clearly uncomfortable.

"Why? I've heard about you and that detective. Did he send you down here? I'm just doing my job. I don't know why he's so insistent that I know something."

I was losing her. She stood, her movements jerky as she pushed back from the table, making the chair grind on the tile floor.

"A man was murdered, Alicia. Right here at the resort. If you know something, or saw something, Penny can't make you keep quiet. You've got to speak up. I'll make sure your job is safe, if that's what you're worried about."

Alicia's eyes filled with tears and her shoulders slumped as she collapsed back into her chair.

"It wasn't Penny. It was someone else. And no, I'm not telling you who. But someone came to me and asked me to clean the gym two nights ago. She said one of her friends was using it and got cut and bled everywhere. She didn't want her friend to get in trouble, so she made me promise to keep it quiet. Am I going to get fired? I was just trying to help."

My mind whirled as I tried to process what she'd just said. Who was the friend she was protecting? I remembered the look she'd shared with Amber. I had a sinking feeling the newest member of the cooking staff was involved.

Chapter Fourteen

By the time my brain and mouth connected, the door behind me swung open and Alicia bolted upright like a frightened rabbit. I didn't even need to turn around to know Penny was behind me. My shoulders tensed as I waited for the verbal barrage to begin.

"Alicia, you're two minutes late for the meeting. If it happens again, I'll have to let Mr. Marsburg know. Punctuality is vital if you're going to succeed on this team."

My teeth ground together so hard I was certain a trip to the dentist was in my very near future. I stood and faced Penny, arms folded across my chest.

"Actually, Penny, I was asking her some questions at Detective Rhodes' request. I'm sure you know how much Mr. Marsburg values our cooperation with the local law enforcement, particularly when a murder occurred on our grounds. Again."

Penny went an ugly color and even though I wanted to wince, to run and hide from the wrath I knew was headed in my direction, I stood firm. I'd just gotten Alicia to talk, and I needed more time with her. There was no way I was going to let Penny bully us.

"Miss Brooks, your interference is not appreciated. We keep a tight schedule in housekeeping, unlike other departments. If you have questions for one of my team members, you need to put in an official request and when that team member has free time, they can accommodate that request. But not while they're on *my* clock. Come, Alicia. Everyone else is waiting."

I stood there, gaping, while Alicia shot me a panicked look and scuttled out of the room, ducking past Penny. I didn't miss the look of unholy glee in Penny's eyes as she turned back to face me. Okay, maybe I'd been a little too optimistic on the whole not letting her bully me thing. I took a deep breath through my nose and pasted on a smile I definitely didn't feel.

"My apologies, Penny. Where can I put in this official request?"

"There's a form in my office. But I can tell you my team is quite busy, so I'm afraid I'm going to ignore any request. If you want to talk to someone, you'll need to do it once they've clocked out for the day, and of course, that might not be convenient for them."

She spun on one of her high heels and marched out of the room, letting the door bang behind her, right in my face. Okay. Well, that went swimmingly. My suspicions about her reared their head again. Was she intentionally making it difficult to get access to her team? Did she have something to do with Mark's death?

I pulled the door open and walked back to the elevator. Somehow, I'd have to catch Alicia before she left for the day. As far as I knew, she didn't live on sight, but maybe Wendy could help me find her address. I would not let Penny stand in the way of uncovering potential evidence.

By the time I made it back to the main floor, the lobby was full of guests, and they did not look happy. Mr. Marsburg was talking over everyone, apologizing for the inconvenience. I looked around for Charlie, but didn't spot her. Danny, however, was hanging out behind one of the large potted plants.

"Danny, what's going on?"

"Shh! I don't want to get involved in this. Where were you?"

"Downstairs, trying to talk to a housekeeper. I think Mark might have been killed in the gym, but before I could ask her any more questions, Penny came in."

Danny snorted.

"How'd that go?"

"As well as you can imagine. I need to talk to Ethan, but I don't think I want to go through that crowd. Why is everyone so angry?"

"The police impounded everyone's sleds and refused to let anyone leave the resort property. They're losing their minds. Why do you think Mark was killed in the gym?"

"Alicia said that another employee here at the resort let one of her friends use the gym. I guess the friend got cut, and they asked Alicia to clean up the blood and keep it quiet. What are the odds of that actually happening?"

"More common than you might think, especially if they were new. Many people try to take advantage of the amenities and show off to their friends. It's happened before. Where did it happen in the gym?"

"I never had time to ask. I wish there was a way to see if there was any blood left behind. They make it look so easy in those crime shows."

Danny brightened and leaned closer.

"I've got an idea. Go to the gym and I'll meet you there. I need to sneak out through the back door and grab something from my cabin."

He was gone before I could ask what was going on. I shrugged and skirted the crowd, avoiding a few of the snowmobilers before they could ask me questions. Typically, I was the first to offer my help, but this was more important.

I used my employee key card to open the gym's door and sat on a bench to wait for Danny. I still hadn't heard how Mark was killed, but I remembered there wasn't any blood on the scene where I'd found him. I pulled out my phone, debating the risks of texting Ethan. Alicia said she'd cleaned up the mess, but did she get it all?

The door swung open and Danny came in, wreathed in smiles and holding what looked like a black wand.

"What's that?"

"A black light. One of my friends got it for me as a gag gift when they heard I was going to work here."

I tilted my head to the side, confused.

"Why?"

"Oh, Eden. I almost hate to tell you. Do you know how some people, um, like to get busy in hotels? Blacklights can pick up the, uh, fluids that are left behind."

"Gross! Do you think it will work on blood?"

"Well, it always seems to work on those shows. That's what made me remember this little thing. Let's see if it works. I think we need to turn off the lights first, though."

I reached behind him and flipped off the light, plunging us into darkness. Within seconds, a purplish glow came from Danny's hand and he held it up.

"This is so cool. I feel like I'm on CSI or something."

He waved the light around and made a sound of disgust when he held it to the wall. Something was glowing brightly.

"Do you think that's blood?" I asked, mesmerized by the effect of the light.

"Er... I don't think so. Back away from the wall. I wish I knew where to look. Did Alicia say what part of the gym she had to clean?"

I looked around the room and shook my head. It was a smaller gym, but there were several pieces of equipment spread across the room.

"No. I suppose we'll have to check the whole place. What's blood supposed to look like under a black light?"

It was dark in the room, but from the silence that came from where Danny was standing, I could almost feel him blushing.

"We might need to look that up."

I rolled my eyes and fired my phone, tapping out a quick search on my browser. As I waited for the results, I snorted.

"It's a good thing I'm not guilty, or I'd be worried about my search history coming to light. Okay, it says here that blood will show up as black unless you spray luminol on it. That's what makes it shine. The only thing that shines without that is saliva, and ew... gross!"

I took another step away from the wall. Danny chuckled as he swept the beam of light around the room.

"Told you. I'm not seeing anything, but it's hard to tell."

"I should have told Ethan about this right away. Now he's going to be mad that we tried to do this on our own."

Danny flicked off the black light, plunging us into complete darkness as I groped around for the light switch. His rue-filled expression was the first thing I saw.

"Sorry, I thought it would help."

I rushed to console him.

"It was a great idea! I didn't know about the luminol thing. I guess we'd better leave this to the professionals."

I led the way out of the room and pulled up short when I ran smack into Ethan. Danny quickly stowed the black light in his back pocket and put on what I could only assume he thought looked like an innocent expression. Unfortunately, the effect was anything but.

"Hi, Ethan. I was just going to look for you."

"Funny, that's what I'm doing. Wendy said she spotted you coming back this way. I was going to let you know your office was free for the rest of the day. What are you two doing back here?"

Was I imagining things or was the look Ethan was leveling at Danny, filled with suspicion and maybe even a little jealousy? I shook off that thought and came clean, relaying what I'd learned from Alicia.

"It sounded suspicious, so I came here to check it out and Danny helped," I said, finishing my story.

Out of the corner of my eye, I could see Danny gesturing wildly, but I ignored him. Ethan straightened, and the friendly expression in his eyes faded.

"So you came back here on your own, even though I'm literally on the premises and potentially disturbed evidence in my murder case?"

Well, when he put it like that... I shook my head as I tried to explain myself.

"We just walked in and used a black light, but this was before we knew you needed luminol to see blood. We touched nothing, and besides, this gym's probably been used a few times since that night. I'm sorry, Ethan."

Danny hung his head and produced the black light from his back pocket.

"Sorry, sir. She's telling the truth, though. You can have this."

Ethan heaved a sigh and shook his head.

"Keep it. I swear you guys are going to be the death of me. I'll get the crime lab boys out here to go over everything with a fine-tooth comb. Often when people think they got all the blood, they don't realize they missed something. You're certain the girl was telling the truth?"

"I am. Danny, can't we pull a record of the keycards that have been used to get in here during the past few days?"

"Sure. It will have all the room numbers in our system."

"What about staff cards?" I asked, as Ethan raised an eyebrow at my question.

"Yep, those too. Why?"

"Just a suspicion. Can you go check that for Ethan, Danny? I want to tell him more about what Alicia said."

Danny gave me a jaunty salute before jogging down the hallway. I waited until he was far enough away and turned back to Ethan.

"Have you already questioned the cooking staff? Amber in particular."

Ethan's eyes searched my face as he nodded.

"Yes, why?"

"It's just a weird coincidence, but she's from the same town as Mark. I remember thinking it was odd. I'd never even heard of it before, and then I heard it twice in the matter of a few hours. When Charlie and I went looking for that sled, we found out his pickup was from the same county as that town. It's not much, but..." I said, trailing off before deciding to forge ahead. "Amber was there in the break room when I went down to talk to Alicia. They shared a look before Amber left. I know I don't have any proof, but I think she was the one with the 'friend' who used the gym. Alicia was certain that Penny wasn't the one who told her not to talk."

Ethan shoved his hands in his pockets and nodded.

"I can definitely bring her back in for questioning. Thanks for digging into this, Eden. But that is where this ends, okay? I appreciate you always trying to help, and I know you've got good instincts, but this is my job. I need to focus on the evidence and not worry that you're getting in over your head."

It stung. Quite a lot. But I knew he had a point. I bit my lip and nodded, swinging my hair over my shoulders.

"I understand."

He smiled, and it was like watching the sun come out after a cloudy day. A tiny part of me wanted to swoon. Okay, it wasn't a tiny part.

"Now that your boss is back, I'll use his office to question Amber. Oh, who's in charge of HR here?"

"Denise, but she's been on leave for about a month. Why?"

"I need the employee records pulled so I can get background on everyone."

"I can do that. I have the main password for our system."

He gave me a wry look before shrugging.

"I guess that's fine. If you could print that off, I'd appreciate it."

"It might be a lot. I could just email you over a file with everything."

"Even better."

We walked back into the lobby together and I noticed with relief that it was empty again. Wendy waved, and I headed in her direction as Ethan stopped by the doors, phone to his ear.

"There you are. I was wondering why you went back there. Everything okay?"

"Yep. I'm going to run to my office to do a few things. It looks like everyone cleared out."

"Mr. Marsburg promised everyone a free weekend of their choice in return for their trouble, and that seemed to help. Whew, it was touch and go there for a minute."

I glanced back and noticed Ethan was still on the phone.

"That's good. I'll be in my office if you need anything. Did Charlie go back to her cabin?"

"Yep. Why?"

"Just checking."

I walked back to my office, thinking about Benny. The odds

were high he'd seen whoever dropped off Mark's body. If I could just get him alone and convince him to talk to me, I could solve this case. I plopped down in my chair and fired up my computer to search through the HR files. Ethan had asked for them, but he hadn't requested I not read them. Maybe I'd find something interesting about our newest employees.

Chapter Fifteen

As I finished compiling all the employee records into one folder for Ethan, a qualm of doubt went through me. I trusted everyone I worked with. They'd welcomed me into their midst and made me a part of the family they'd built. I didn't know Amber or Alicia, but that didn't mean they were guilty.

I shook my head and finished dragging the last of the files into the folder before compressing it and loading my email program. I needed to get these sent over before I changed my mind. After all, if they were innocent, they had nothing to worry about. Right? I sighed and typed up a quick email to Ethan and attached the files.

Once they were gone, the feeling in my stomach unfortunately stuck around. I pushed back from my desk and went to my small window to look out. Ice fanned out from the edges, framing the resort in all of its wintery glory. I was truly lucky to have found a place like this. If it hadn't been for Hannah Murphy, I'd still be working at an actor's estate, desperately unhappy.

Thoughts of Hannah and her merry band of cats made me smile. It had been a while since I checked up with her. I walked back to my desk, sat down, and dialed her number while checking my watch. It was just before quitting time, but Hannah worked odd hours in her job as the crime beat reporter for the Post down in Golden Hills, Colorado. It rang twice before Hannah's warm voice came onto the line.

"Eden! We were just thinking about you."

I heard her cat's delicate voice in the background and my smile deepened. Hannah shared my ability to speak to cats, and she was still helping me come to terms with my new reality. I didn't understand how it happened, and to be honest, I didn't want to think about it too much in the fear it might disappear some day.

"Hi Hannah. Hi Razzy. I didn't catch you two at a bad time, did I?"

"Not at all. I'm driving home. The boys will be sad they missed you."

"Are you all still planning on coming up to see us?"

"Absolutely. There's a festival that's coming up, and Ben's detective business is really taking off, but we'll definitely make time this spring to come up there. I've heard the wildflower season is incredible."

"Really? I didn't know that. There's so much snow up here it feels like Spring will never come. I'm not used to life in the mountains."

"It will get better..."

She trailed off as Razzy let out an exasperated meow.

"Eden, what's wrong? I can tell something's bothering you and it's not just the snow. You can tell us."

"Well, Razzy. You're not wrong. There's been another murder."

Their twin gasps echoed through the phone.

"Oh no. Not an employee? I mean, not that I want it to be a guest or anything, but are your friends okay? The cats?"

"We're all fine. There's a recent addition to the clowder. My friend Charlie is taking care of him while he recovers from his sickness. It was a guest from the snowmobiling competition."

I took them both through the facts before diving into my suspicions. As a crime reporter, Hannah had developed years of skills in sorting through information to solve cases. Add in her amazing abilities, and her seemingly endless supply of spot-on intuition, and she was just the person I needed to talk to. By the time I was done, I felt better, even though I was still very much in the dark.

"Wow. You've got your hands full. What's Dave's last name again?"

"Shepherd. Do you think you might be able to pull some background on him?"

"Of course. I'll do it when I get home. Gus and Rudy would love to help. And yes, you would too, Razzy. That goes without saying."

"I could also send over some employee files if you're not too busy. I can't shake the feeling that it's not a coincidence that Amber and Mark are from the same town. I wish I'd gotten the plate number from the pickup that tried to force me off the road."

"What?"

Hannah's screech made me yank my phone away from my ear for a moment before putting it back.

"Oh, I might have left that out. It happened when we were bringing Benny, that's the new cat, back from the vet. It was a black pickup with tinted windows. Ethan said it matched a description of a pickup stolen from Nebraska, but no one's seen it since."

"Eden, you need to be careful. I wish we could get up there to help you."

"I'll be okay. You've got your hands full down there. Just talking to you is a tremendous help to me. You always know the right things to say."

"Ha. You don't know me that well, then. I'm the world's most awkward person half the time. Send those files over and we'll get to work. Ben's got some new software. He might be able to trace that pickup."

"You are the best. I can't wait to see you guys again. Give Rudy and Gus my love. You too, Razzy girl."

"See you soon, Eden. Watch your back. Tell Jasper we all said hi," Razzy said.

"Oh, that reminds me. Do you remember Luna?"

Razzy's voice was a little flatter than usual.

"Yes. Why?"

"She and Oscar just had three kittens. They're staying with me during this cold snap. They're adorable."

There was a pause on the other end of the line and I couldn't help but get the feeling Razzy wasn't a big fan of Luna. Hannah's voice came back on.

"How adorable. You'll have to send us pictures. I'm almost home. I'll text you if I find anything out."

"Thanks, Hannah. Talk to you soon."

I ended the call, still curious. Maybe Jasper would know the story of why the two queens didn't get along. I shut down my computer and grabbed my bag. I'd worked through lunch and my stomach let me know it was not amused by that one bit.

Wendy was on the phone when I walked out and got into my coat. I waved to her and headed out, debating on whether to stop at my cabin before going to the dining hall. I spotted Charlie walking ahead of me and remembered I needed to talk to Benny.

"Charlie! Wait up," I called, taking a shortcut through the deeper snow to catch up with her.

"Hey, Eden! Ready for dinner?"

My mind raced for an excuse to go into her cabin alone, even as guilt made my stomach twist.

"Do you mind if I borrow that fuzzy sweater of yours? I'm freezing and all my hoodies are dirty."

"Of course you can. Do you want me to go back with you?"

"If you've got your keys handy, I can just grab it. You know it's stuffed baked potato night, and that means Danny will be lying in wait to get the biggest one."

Charlie's face lit up, and she tossed me her keys.

"We can't let that happen. My place is a disaster, but say hi to Benny. I was planning on saving him some leftovers."

She kept going, and I turned back to the cabins, feeling sick that I'd just lied to my best friend. Would she believe me if I told her? Charlie was open-minded, but maybe that was asking too much. As I put the key in the lock, I promised myself this was the last time I'd do something like this. It just felt wrong.

I turned the light on and jumped as Benny hissed, his eyes adjusting to the bright light.

"I'm so sorry, Benny. Are you feeling better?"

His greenish eyes narrowed as he backed up towards his bed. His ears were flattened down on his head, giving him a very unapproachable look. I swallowed hard and sank down into a crouch.

"I won't hurt you, Benny. I promise. I'm sorry if I startled you by walking in so fast."

I waited, but he didn't respond, never taking his eyes off as he backed away, hackles up. I sat down with a thud as my mind raced on how I could make him more comfortable with my presence.

He shifted back and forth, tucking and un-tucking his paws. From my experience with Jasper, cats only tucked their paws when they felt safe. I needed to assure this poor cat that I didn't want to hurt him.

"Are you feeling any better? Is there anything I can get you?"

Silence. I kept talking, hoping to put him at ease. I told him the story of how I'd found Jasper and nursed him back to health. His greenish eyes closed as I talked about finding Mark's body and our troubles with figuring out who killed him. By the time I was done, he'd finally relaxed. But he still said nothing.

I checked my watch and realized way too much time had passed since I'd left Charlie on her way to the dining hall. If Benny had anything to say, he didn't seem inclined to share it with me. I heaved a sigh and got back to my feet, watching as his eyes flared back to alertness.

"Thanks for listening, Benny. Maybe we can talk again some other time."

I was almost at the door when I heard his voice for the first time. It was low, barely audible, and scratchy.

"It's not natural, you know. Having a human understand us. It takes some getting used to. Fig talked about you. She said I could trust you."

I paused and nodded, slowly turning around.

"You can, Benny. I promise I would never hurt you. I'm sorry we had to take you to the vet, but you were very sick."

He coughed, but it sounded better than it had the day before. He shifted and tucked his paws, forming a loaf shape.

"In my experience, humans are not to be trusted. The only thing they're good for is yelling and throwing things at poor helpless cats who are just trying to live their lives. Tell me why I should help you when all humans have ever done is make my life miserable."

My heart hurt at the bitterness in his tone and made me wish there was a way I could wave a magic wand and make all stray cats safe and loved. Tears pricked at the corner of my eyes.

"We're not all bad, Benny. Look at Charlie. There's something about her you like."

His whiskers quivered, and he made eye contact, his expression carefully guarded.

"I don't know why. She feels familiar to me. Like I've known her before."

"Maybe somehow you have. Anything is possible. She's my dearest friend, and such a good person. I'm glad you let her take you in. I understand if you don't want to help. I can't blame you. I won't keep pestering you. It's more important that you get well."

Silence filled Charlie's cabin as we looked at each other. Finally, Benny heaved a sigh, hitching a little at the end.

"There were two of them. They were very loud, arguing back and forth. I'd been looking for a warm place to sleep when they showed up, so I hid."

Nervous excitement coursed through my muscles, but I stayed still so I wouldn't scare the poor cat.

"Do you think you'd recognize them if you saw them again?"

He gave a kitty shrug of his shoulders and looked down.

"My sniffer hasn't been working. They were all covered up, so I don't know if I'd know them by sight. But maybe if I heard their voices, I'd know them. I think one of them was a woman, but I'm not sure. That night is hazy in my mind. I'll try to remember, though. For Charlie's sake. If there are murderous humans around, she could be at risk. I like her."

I crouched down near Benny. This time, he didn't shy away.

"Thank you, Benny. That's very helpful. Focus on getting better and let us worry about the killers. Charlie's planning on bringing you some treats tonight. Is there anything in particular you'd like?"

"Whatever she brings will be fine. She doesn't know, does she? That you can talk to us."

"No. She doesn't. It's not a common thing and..."

"Secrets have a way of destroying even the closest friendships. Remember that, human."

He closed his eyes, shutting off our communication, and I stood, heart heavy. He was right. Eventually, I had to come clean. The longer I put it off, the worse it would be once Charlie found out.

"I'll try, Benny. I'll try. Thank you for talking with me."

I was so preoccupied, I almost forgot to grab the fuzzy sweater I'd used as an excuse to talk to Benny. I sorted through the pile of clothes on her bed and found it, hugging it to my chest. I walked out, closing the door softly behind me. Maybe tonight I'd tell her. If I could find the courage.

Chapter Sixteen

Even though the food was delicious, as always, I just couldn't enjoy it. My mind kept twisting itself into knots, going over Edgar's claims, my suspicions about Amber, and, of course, how I was going to tell Charlie my secret. Luckily, everyone else seemed to carry on as normal and didn't notice I was more quiet than normal.

"Was Benny sleeping when you grabbed the sweater? I'm worried about him."

Charlie turned towards me as she took the last bite of her stuffed baked potato, eyes bright. I nodded, feeling even more miserable.

"He seems like he's feeling better. We need to make sure he gets plenty of protein. That will help him fight off that virus and heal quicker."

"I already tucked some filet into my napkin, and I'm sure Luke will have some extras, too. Do you mind if I go with you again tonight? I really enjoyed that."

I nodded and tried to smile, hoping she wouldn't pick up on how miserable I was. Her eyes stayed locked with mine for a moment before she turned back towards Danny.

"Are you going to finish that steak?" she asked as Danny automatically hunched over his plate, fork at the ready.

"You've gotta be kidding me. You already ate your steak and that entire potato and now you want mine, too?"

He winked at her before slicing off a sizable chunk and handing it over.

"Thanks. And it's for Benny, not me."

"I figured, silly. Anyway, that's my second steak and I probably shouldn't eat it all. Ooo, are they putting out cobbler for dessert? I can't wait for the late summer when we'll have some peach cobbler. Eden, that's the absolute ultimate dessert. What were you guys whispering about?"

"We were just talking about going to feed the cats," I said, choking down a little more of my potato before giving up.

"I'll go with. Until this is figured out, I don't think it's safe for you two to be wandering the grounds alone."

Charlie and I exchanged a glance before I looked back at Danny. His neck flushed under my scrutiny.

"Did Ethan ask you to do that?"

"No. Well, sorta. But it was my idea, and he thought it was a good one. He's going over the key card data tonight. By tomorrow, we should know who accessed the gym that night."

"What's this?"

I quickly filled Charlie in about what we'd learned and she looked over at the kitchen staff, eyes wide.

"You don't think she had something to do with it, do you? She seems pretty nice. And normal. I wouldn't peg her as a murderer."

"Charlie! Quit staring. I don't know, yet, but we have few leads and so far, this is the most promising. I'm gonna give Jasper and Luna the rest of my potato. Are you ready to go feed the cats? It's been a long day."

If Charlie was surprised by my sudden desire to get out of the dining hall, she hid it well. She stored her wrapped up food bundle in her coat pocket and met me at the tray station. Danny hustled over and grabbed a bowl of cobbler, eating it as he walked over to us.

"Charming," Charlie said as Danny's cheeks bulged out.

"Hey, don't knock for the road cobbler until you've tried it. So, what do we do? Grab some food and head out there?"

"Pretty much," I said, looking for Luke. "Let me see what they've got for the cats tonight."

I poked my head back into the kitchen, where I spotted Luke and Amber in deep conversation. He noticed me and stepped back, smiling.

"Eden, do you mind if …?"

I held up a hand, cutting him off.

"No worries, Luke. Charlie and Danny are helping tonight. I figured you were still tied up with the meal prep for the guests. With any luck, they'll know who the killer is by tomorrow and everyone can go home."

I watched Amber's eyes to see how she'd react, but she just stared back at me. Maybe it had been a bad idea, but I had to try. Luke handed me a tray heaped with the gristle they'd cut off the steaks before serving them, and I could only imagine the delight of the clowder once they discovered this feast.

He followed me out after another quick word with Amber and gave Danny the other tray.

"What am I, chopped liver?" Charlie asked with a grin.

"You can carry my road cobbler, but no sneaking bites. I know exactly how much is left."

"It's like you never met me."

She held open the doors for us and we began the trek towards the forest. I let their banter wash over me as I plodded through the snow, feeling as though it were a metaphor for the state of this case. I was up to my knees in theories and suspicions, but nothing was clear.

We made it to the clearing, and Danny and Charlie watched as the cats streamed out of the trees to meet us. Fig bounded into view, pulling up short when she saw them. Her yellow eyes bored into mine, passing along a message, even in the dark, that came through loud and clear. She had something to say to me.

I spread out the food for the cats and eased in her direction, hoping Charlie and Danny were talking loudly enough they wouldn't hear us. I knelt near the brown cat and turned my back towards my friends.

"What's up?"

"Willow has discovered something that she thought you should see. I looked and I think it's important. Someone's hidden a large vehicle in the trees, right in the middle of one of our hunting trails. She'll lead you to it. It needs to go. Its stink is scaring off the prey, and it's already been hard enough to find anything to eat."

"I'll go look at it. Is Oscar okay? I didn't see him last night, and Luna was worried."

"He's fine, but owly. The hunting is so poor he came up empty pawed last night. He's angry that I wouldn't let him take from the clowder's stores, but I know you're feeding Luna well. He's over there, sulking," she said, waving her tail in the direction of a nearby shrub.

I squinted through the darkness, but I couldn't pick Oscar's black coat up. What I wouldn't give for cat vision, especially at night.

"Benny's doing better. Thank you for helping us get him."

"Good. Please get rid of that vehicle if you can."

She stalked off, tail waving, as she approached the food. Just like Jasper, she always waited until all the other cats ate before enjoying her portion. I spotted Willow's mottled form against the snow as she jogged towards me.

"Ready, Eden? It's not far."

I looked back at my friends, who were still talking, standing quite close to one another. I smiled and left them to their moment. Maybe Danny had finally worked up enough courage to ask Charlie out.

"Let's go, sweetheart. Are you warm enough?"

"I'm fine," she said, whiskers quirked before she leapt behind a tree.

I struggled to keep up, but eventually, Willow stopped and waited for me to catch up, panting heavily.

"I wish I was as agile as you. How much further?"

"It's right there. I forget you humans can't smell things like we do."

I squinted again and finally caught a bit of chrome gleaming as the clouds moved, letting the moonlight through. Even in the dark, I knew we'd found the pickup that threatened us on the road. What on earth was it doing back here in the trees?

I looked around before going closer, phone ready to take some pictures to send to Ethan. The license plate was gone, but this had to be the right vehicle.

"Your friends are coming," Willow said, her voice a whisper. "I've got to go. See you later, Eden."

Loud footsteps crashed through the trees and I heard Charlie shouting for me.

"Over here, guys. You'll never believe it. It's the pickup."

Charlie's stocking hat was askew as she came to a stop next to me, giving me a funny look.

"How did you find this?"

Sweat trickled down my back as I struggled to come up with an excuse.

"I thought I saw something gleaming through the trees, so I went to check it out. This is the right one, isn't it?"

"Dang, that's a nice pickup," Danny said, walking closer to it. "That's gotta be worth at least sixty thousand."

He reached a hand out to touch it.

"Don't! Ethan's going to need to get the prints off it."

"It sure looks like the one we saw," Charlie said, never taking her eyes off my face. "That's pretty amazing. You were able to see it all the way from where we were standing."

I glanced away and nodded.

"Well, we'd better let Ethan know. My phone isn't great at taking night photos, but it will have to do."

"I'll stand back over here and use my flashlight to light it up," Danny offered, backing up through the snow. "That should help. You can send him a GPS pin at our location to make it easier to find it."

"Great idea on both counts."

Charlie remained quiet, her arms wrapped around her middle, while I took my pictures. Danny moved back a little more to make sure the light hit the pickup body just right. I pulled open my text app and quickly typed out a message to Ethan. The thrill of the cat's find coursed through me as I hit send.

"Alright, let me get a copy of our location and then we should be good. I wonder what's inside the pickup?"

Charlie crept closer and peeked inside the window, carefully leaning so she didn't accidentally touch it.

"I see nothing in there. I wonder if they stowed it in here and wiped it clean from prints. It's stolen, right?"

"That's what Ethan said."

I was barely listening as I copied the link from my map program to send. A loud yowl from within the forest nearly made me drop my phone as I spun around.

"Danny! Look out!"

I turned at Charlie's shout, just in time to see a tall man behind Danny bring something down on the top of his head. He fell like a stone and my heart hammered as two more figures joined the first. A beam of light hit my face, and my eyes closed automatically as my hands flew up to shade them.

"Hand over the phones. Both of you."

Charlie slowly walked towards me, hands in the air as my heart tried to hammer out of my chest. A sick feeling spread through my stomach as I looked at Danny. He wasn't moving. Had they killed him? Charlie whimpered as she slowly took her phone out of her pocket and held it up. I jabbed my thumb towards what I hoped was the send button on my text before holding mine up.

"Toss them over here. Now!"

I debated winging my phone at the man's head, but changed my mind as I noticed the other two had what looked like weapons trained on us. Floaters danced in my eyes as they tried to adjust to the bright light still being shined in my face. Charlie tossed her phone first and then I threw mine, landing it deliberately short of the man in front of us.

I put my hands back up in the air as my mind raced. Had

Amber tipped them off that we'd be in this part of the forest, or was it a coincidence? I took a step forward and mustered my courage. With any luck, Ethan was already on his way here, and he'd know exactly where we were. Right now, I needed to make sure Danny was still alive and keep the men talking.

"Stop right there. Not one more step."

I turned towards the man who spoke and gasped. I knew that voice.

Chapter Seventeen

W hile I'd thought Edgar was innocent, I hadn't expected to
have it confirmed quite like this. They kept the bright light
on our faces, so I still couldn't see who the other two people were,
but I knew Dave Shepherd was one of them.

"Why? Why did you do it?" I asked, unable to keep quiet. "You
could have found another job. I'm certain that being on Mark's
team would have meant you'd be very popular with his competitors.
Especially if you knew how to rig sleds to ensure they'd win. Like
you did for Mark."

Dave let out a jagged laugh and moved closer.

"How did you know about that? Listening in at doors, you little
snoop?"

I narrowed my eyes in indignation. I wasn't a snoop. Well, not
this time anyway. I couldn't throw Edgar under the bus, though.
What if they killed us and went straight for him? What if I hadn't
sent our location to Ethan after all?

"Let's just say it wasn't a big secret you were fired. But murder?
It seems a little extreme."

Charlie whimpered as Danny moved a little. He wasn't dead! I
needed to keep them talking and pray I'd buy us enough time to get

rescued. There was no way the two of us could take on three people with guns.

The second person joined Dave, moving to stand shoulder to shoulder with him. The beam of light hit her face, and I looked between them, finally seeing the resemblance.

"Amber! You're his sister, aren't you?"

"Well, look who gets a prize," Amber said, sneering. "You should see your face. It's a riot. You didn't even look this scared when I pointed the gun at you from the pickup. Too bad your famed intuition was a little delayed, huh, princess? Guess you're not so smart after all."

"That was you?" Charlie asked, her voice cracking. "Why Amber? I thought you were one of us. We welcomed you with open arms."

"This one's waking up. What do you want me to do with him?"

Dave's eyes never left mine as he shouted to the third person.

"Get him over here. Let's line them up in front of the pickup. I wouldn't want one of them to think they could escape."

The other man hauled Danny to his feet, cursing as Danny vomited all over his boots.

"Oh man, that's just gross."

Charlie whimpered again as Danny was propelled forward. He tripped over his feet and went down hard, spraying snow everywhere. Dave cursed and walked forward, hauling Danny upward again. I grabbed Charlie's arm as I realized where Danny had fallen, right over where my phone lay in the snow. Had he grabbed it?

"Line 'em up. I don't know why you were so worried about these guys, Amber. They're pathetic."

Anger swelled my chest but the barrel of the gun shoved into it quickly deflated it. I backed until I felt the cold chrome from the front of the pickup dig into my back. This was not the way I wanted to go out, and it was not what I wanted for my friends.

"Look, let them go. I was the one poking around, not them. They're innocent," I said, hating the pleading tone I could hear in my voice.

"Ha. Not buying it," Amber said. "You three are thick as thieves. I'm sure you already told them everything. What are we waiting for, Dave? Let's get rid of them and get out of here. We can't use the pickup, but we can use my car. No one will think to look for it. You saw how surprised she was when saw me. I'm not a suspect."

"Hang on a minute," Dave ground out. "Don't tell me what we do. I'm running this show, okay? Not you."

Hmm. Sibling rivalry might come in handy if I could pit the two of them against each other. Who was the third man? He stood close to Amber, and his face was vaguely familiar. He sneered at me.

"What are you waiting for?" he asked. "It's fricking cold out here, man. We need to hit the road."

"I want to find out exactly what they know. I've heard the little one is cozy with the detective in town. We need to ask them a few questions and then I'll pop them, okay? I'm trying to ensure we can have a clean break."

"Well, hurry it up," Amber grumbled, looking around. "This place gives me the creeps. There are all these cats lurking around. You know how I feel about cats. Maybe we can pop a few of them off, too. I should've snuck something into the food that sap Luke was always putting aside for them."

My opinion of Amber bottomed out. Cat haters were the worst of the worst in my books.

"Luke is not a sap! He's kind, which is more than I can say for any of you," I said, anger blazing back to life. "And one of those feral cats is worth eighty of you. At least they don't kill innocent people and twist everyone up in lies."

Amber rolled her eyes and turned away towards the other man. He sneered at me again.

"Enough. I want to know everything you know, everything that cop has told you. Are we suspects?"

"She's just going to lie," Amber said. "I don't know why you're wasting your time."

"Thought of that, already, sis," Dave said, reaching for Charlie and placing the barrel of the gun at her temple. "Now, Eden. Be a good girl and tell me everything you know or you'll get to watch your little friend breathe her last."

My hands shook as Charlie's panicked eyes met mine. Danny groaned deep in his chest and moved towards Charlie automatically.

"Down, lover boy," Amber said, training her gun on Danny. "I've heard you were sweet on her. Maybe you'd like to go first."

"Stop this. I'll tell you everything," I said, desperate to stall them. "I told Ethan you'd been fired, and my suspicions about you. But he has nothing concrete. Just the fact you destroyed the footprints around Mark's body, and you had a motive for wanting him dead. As far as I know, there's no evidence."

"Keep talking. There's more. I see it on your face," Dave said, leaning so close I could smell his rancid breath.

"I suspected Amber was the one who got Alicia to clean up the mess you made in the gym when you killed Mark. We don't know how you got him in there, or why. Ethan got forensics to search for blood stains. They'll be able to tell if it belonged to Mark. Let her go!"

Charlie's expression would haunt me for the rest of my life as Dave jammed the barrel into her tender skin. I held up my hands.

"I'm telling you everything I know. He doesn't know the pickup is tied to you, and he doesn't know the two of you are related."

"Who were you texting when we showed up?" Amber asked, eyes gleaming in the moonlight. "Don't even try to deny it. I saw you. You found the pickup, and you texted your little boyfriend, didn't you?"

I swallowed hard. We were running out of time. If Danny didn't grab my phone when he fell, they'd find it and they'd know help was on the way. But if I lied, I had a horrible feeling Dave would shoot Charlie in retaliation.

"I texted Ethan about the pickup. But it's late. He might not have even seen it. If you leave now, you'll get away."

Dave looked over his shoulder at the other man and motioned with his head.

"Tim, find her phone. If you're lying, your little friend gets it. Are you ready to have her blood on your hands?"

Tim slogged through the snow, cursing loudly, and I watched as he kicked the snow away from where we'd tossed our phones. I prayed he wouldn't find it. Danny brushed my shoulder with his, but I didn't dare look. I couldn't pull my eyes away.

"Got one of them," he said, holding up Charlie's phone, encased in its colorful case. "I can't find the other one."

"Look harder. I swear, I've got to do everything myself. Don't move," Dave said, snarling as he pushed Charlie forward.

I grabbed her arm while Danny took her other hand.

"Are you okay?"

Charlie nodded, her movements jerky.

"For now."

Amber kept her gun leveled at us while the two men kicked through the snow, their voices getting louder as they failed to find it. She turned her attention to us and cocked her head to the side, looking at Danny.

"They didn't take your phone, did they? Son of a... Dave! Get back over here. You forgot to grab this one's phone. He's probably already called the cops."

Danny blanched as Dave came sprinting over. Charlie pressed close to Danny and I could only pray he passed her my phone.

"I didn't bring it," Danny said, holding up his hands. "I left it in my cabin. I don't like to bring it when I eat dinner since it distracts me. You can check."

Dave yanked him forward and patted him down, turning out every pocket in Danny's coat.

"Where's your phone?" he said, finally turning towards me. "What did you do with it?"

I pointed towards the snow where I'd thrown it.

"You asked me to throw it and I did. You saw me. Look, if you leave now, you'll be able to get away. Don't add three more murders to your troubles. They have nothing on you. Leave now and we won't say anything. I promise."

He gave a twisted laugh and shook his head. The wind kicked up, blowing snow around.

"Good try, but no dice. Tim, have you found it yet?"

"No, I'm still looking."

"Amber, go help your idiot boyfriend. I don't know why I convinced Mark to give him a job. He can't find his rear with both hands, let alone anything else."

Amber gave me a look filled to the brim with suspicion, but she did as her brother ordered, turning her back to us. We were down to one gun on us again, but I was too paralyzed by the thought of one of my friends dying to make a move. Was Ethan coming? Had he seen my text? He'd never find us out here. I tried to appeal to Dave's conscience once more.

"At least let them go. I'm the one you want, not them. My friends are innocent."

"Not happening. They know too much. You all do. Tim?"

"Still looking."

Dave turned back to me and I could see the madness in his eyes as he trained them on me.

"I've had about enough. Mark Chesney deserved to die for what he did. And you three do, too."

"Firing you was worth killing?"

"That's not all he did! He threw my little sister away like trash and laughed about it right in front of me. He was scum! He threatened to make sure I never worked in the industry again. I was the only reason he won!"

The last puzzle piece slipped into place.

"He didn't know he was cheating. He thought it was his skill that won races, but it wasn't, was it? At least not entirely. You supercharged the sleds and sold that information to Edgar. When Mark realized he was a cheater, he fired you and threatened to go public with the information."

"He actually said he was going to give up all of his wins and prize money, and take me to court to pay back the wages he'd paid me. I worked hard for that money! I made sure he was the best. He didn't deserve me and he didn't deserve my sister! When I think about everything he did to our family, I couldn't take it anymore. I saw my opportunity to rid the world of that guy, and I'm glad I did it. He always went to the gym at the crack of dawn. He bragged that was why he always won. He didn't even know it was only because of me. Me! He was so wrapped up in his own reflection, he didn't even see me until it was too late. Tim!"

"Nothing, boss. I'm sorry. There's just too much snow. Get rid of them and let's get out of here. We're wasting time."

Dave turned back to us and for a split second, I saw everyone and everything I cared about encapsulated in his eyes. What would happen to Jasper if I was gone? What would happen to Benny and all the other cats? I couldn't go down without a fight.

A noise roared overhead and a bright light lit up the forest with blinding intensity. Snow swirled into a vortex as I grabbed for Charlie and Danny to pull them down on the ground.

"Get down on the ground and put your hands over your heads," boomed a familiar voice from the trees.

For a second, I thought Dave would comply. I looked up from where I'd landed in the snow as Dave cackled madly and began shooting upward, towards the helicopter hovering over us. Bullets sprayed as I buried my head in the snow, clinging to both of my friends as chaos reigned over our heads.

Chapter Eighteen

I t felt as if the world was ending as I lay face down in the snow, trying to make sense of the surrounding cacophony. A sizzling sound near my head drew my attention, and I spotted the long barrel of a rifle, Dave's rifle, melting the snow. Had he surrendered? The whir of the chopper's blades overhead drowned out all the other sounds. I squeezed my eyes shut and prayed that no one was hit by a bullet.

"Eden! They gave up! Look over there."

I rolled to my side as Charlie shouted in my ear and saw three figures kneeling in the snow, their hands over their heads as Ethan and several other officers swarmed around. We'd been saved!

"Ladies, if you'll slowly stand and move over here," a voice said, coming from the trees.

Danny snorted and levered himself upright.

"I'm not even mad. I'm just glad we're all alive. Charlie, you didn't get hit, did you?"

He felt up and down her body, patting her legs with panicky movements.

"I'm fine, silly," Charlie said, her voice strangled. "I think we're actually all fine. I can't believe it."

"This way, please," the voice ordered again.

We trooped through the snow and I looked over my shoulder one more time at the rifle in the snow. We'd come so close I almost couldn't believe we were alive. It felt like I was walking in a dream as I joined my friends in the trees.

"Please stay here until Detective Rhodes is done with the shooters. We'll need to get statements from you. He already let us know your identities, but we'll need to confirm everything."

I nodded, attention back towards Ethan, who was herding the three killers towards the helicopter. Charlie leaned close.

"I didn't think Valewood had a police helicopter."

"It's from our search and rescue team, ma'am," the officer said, nodding at her. "Detective Rhodes requested it when it was taking too long to find you."

"That means he never got my last text. Danny, did you fall on my phone?"

He nodded proudly before moving his hand behind Charlie. She squawked as he pulled my phone out of her back pocket.

"Got it right here. I'm glad I was thinking clearly enough to do that. Dang, my head hurts."

"That's right," Charlie said, feeling along his scalp. "Officer, we need paramedics. He was hit on the head and fell unconscious. Is he going to be okay?"

"Paramedics are on their way. Rhodes is coming over here now."

I glanced at my phone and saw what would have been my last text, still sitting there, unsent. How had he found us?

"Eden..." Ethan jogged towards us, his face tight underneath his black stocking hat. "You're okay."

"I'm fine. We're all okay. I can't believe they gave up."

"They ran out of bullets, or I think it would have ended differently. Officer Samuels, if you'll accompany the suspects, that will be great. I'll take my vehicle back to the station. We'll need to use the county jail. Our local one won't be enough."

"Will do, boss."

Once Officer Samuels was gone, Ethan began looking through the brush in the surrounding trees.

"Did they throw something over there?" I asked, curious.

"No, your cat was with us and I'm scared to death something happened to him," Ethan said, pausing in his movements for a second. "I went to your cabin to find you, and he was yowling his head off. I opened the door, which you really need to lock, and he shot out of there and headed towards the forest. He led me right to you."

Panic jolted through my heart and my legs shook as I walked towards Ethan, shouting for Jasper. Oh God, what if a stray bullet had found Jasper? It didn't take long before I heard his familiar rusty-sounded meow. Relief flooded through me so intensely I fell to my knees in the snow. Jasper poked his head out from a nearby shrub and winked at me. Tears fell as I scooped him into my arms and held him close.

"Oh thank goodness, he's okay," Ethan said, standing next to me awkwardly. "I don't know what I'm going to put in my report, but if it hadn't been for him..."

I nodded, burying my face in Jasper's fur as my friends joined us, talking over each other.

"I heard a yowl. Right before you got hit. The cats were trying to warn us, I swear it," Charlie said.

"She's right," I said, struggling to get to my feet until Ethan's hand supported my elbow. "Thank you. I think it was Willow, but I'm uncertain."

"Well, she saved our lives. And so did this little guy," Charlie said, placing a loud kiss on Jasper's forehead, much to his consternation. "So, we need to get Danny to the hospital. I'm worried that the blow to his head scrambled what little brains he's got in there."

Ethan straightened, and he looked at Danny before flicking on his flashlight. He held it up to Danny's eyes, who winced and stepped back.

"Your pupils are okay, but you should still get checked out. Does anyone want to tell me what happened here?"

All three of us started talking at once. Charlie waved her arms around, recounting the most dramatic parts of our story, while Danny corrected her. Ethan's warm eyes they landed on me, and he heaved a sigh.

"Let's do it one at a time, guys. Eden?"

I took a shaky breath and held Jasper closer. Even though I knew he wasn't the biggest fan of long snuggles, he lay, content, in my arms, giving me the strength to recount everything that happened. By the time I was done, I felt physically and emotionally wrung-out, like a dishrag after cleaning up the dishes from a huge Thanksgiving meal.

Charlie nodded and spoke up.

"Yep, that's pretty much what happened. Danny's quick thinking bought us time while they tried to find Eden's phone. They weren't the smartest criminals, though, were they? I'm still going to have nightmares for months, though. I thought we were done for."

Ethan's face was unreadable as he looked at us. His gaze settled on Jasper, and he reached over to stroke the cat's head.

"I still can't believe it. I hate to think about how it could have ended if I hadn't gone to your cabin first. You're very lucky, Eden."

I could only nod in silent agreement, still too overwhelmed to speak.

"Can we go inside? I'm freezing," Charlie said, wiping her nose with her hand. "I don't know if I'll ever get warm."

"It's shock. Let's get you guys to the paramedics."

We set off together, but Charlie caught my sleeve and slowed my steps. Once Danny and Evan were far enough ahead, she spoke.

"So, you saw the pickup gleaming under the moonlight, huh?"

I realized I'd told Ethan the truth, that Willow led me to the pickup, when I'd said something else to Charlie. I realized that now was as good a time as any to come clean. I could only hope my friend would understand.

"I'm sorry, Charlie. I've been lying to you," I said, lowering my voice so they couldn't hear us up ahead. "I know what I'm about to say sounds pretty crazy, but I hope you'll believe me."

"Well, that's not a great start," Charlie said, but she tucked her hand in my arm as we walked. "Let me have it."

"Before I came here, Hannah Murphy, I've told you about her before, asked me to look after the feral cats. She's the one who helped me get the job. A few days after I started here, I found out that... Well, I discovered I can talk to cats."

Charlie wrinkled her nose and shrugged.

"Duh. we all can. I hear you talking to the cats all the time. It's sweet."

"No, that's not what I mean. I literally talk to cats. And they talk back. I can understand them, Charlie. I talk to them just like I talk to you."

She was silent for a moment before laughing so loudly Danny and Ethan turned around, staring at us. She trailed off as soon as she realized I wasn't laughing.

"You're not kidding, are you?"

"No. I'm not. I've wanted to tell you for a long time, but... I didn't want you to think I'm crazy. You're the best friend I've ever had, and so I waited. Until now. It's gone on too long, and you probably hate me for lying to you. Benny told me I needed to tell you, and he was right. He said secrets destroy friendships."

She pulled me to a stop and looked at me, her face solemn.

"I could never hate you, Eden Brooks. Never say that. Benny said that to you?" she asked.

I watched as comprehension dawned on her face. Her eyes sharpened.

"That's why you wanted to go back to my cabin tonight. It wasn't to borrow a sweater, it was so you could talk to Benny, alone."

I nodded, miserable, and started walking again. She hustled to catch up.

"I did. I'm sorry. If it's any consolation, I hated every time I had to tell you something that wasn't true. I don't blame you if you don't want to talk to me again. I can leave the resort and try to find a different job. But I have to look after the clowder. I promised. They're my family."

"I'm your family, too," Charlie said, shaking her head. "And so is Danny, for what that's worth. Does he know?"

"No. You're the only one I've told."

"Ethan doesn't know either?"

"Nope."

"Wow. Awkward. So, cool, you can talk to cats. That's pretty cool, actually. What do they sound like?"

Jasper let out a huffing sound that I knew was his laugh.

"I told you that you worry too much. See, look how well she took it."

"What did he just say?"

"He said that I worry too much and I should've had more faith in you. Well, I'm paraphrasing that bit. It's true, though."

"Duh. We're besties. I bet their voices sound kinda like how they meow. Like Jasper probably has a raspy voice."

"Kind of. You're taking this pretty well."

"Well, I've known something was up for a while. I was worried you had some deep, awful secret or something. This is actually pretty mild."

I blinked, surprised.

"Really? That's all you're going to say?"

"It's obvious you have a way with cats. I mean, look at the way even that scary brown cat comes to you. Weirdly, it makes sense. Besides, I grew up watching Sabrina and wishing it was true. Oh! Do you think I'll ever be able to do that too? I mean, is it catching? Can you like cough on me or something? That would be so cool if I could do it, too."

I relaxed as the tension from our ordeal and my fears about telling her melted away.

"I don't think it works that way, but you never know. Hannah can talk to her cats. She says she thought there was something about me when we met. That's why she asked me to come here. I think she knew somehow that I shared her abilities."

"So cool. So, what does Benny think of me? Hey, is that why you know all their names? You didn't name them, did you? Those are their actual names. I just thought you had a fantastic imagination and an endless supply of cat names."

"Yep, those are their actual names. Benny likes you. He says you remind him of someone. He still doesn't like me, though."

"He'll come around. You don't think he's my Benjamin, do you? I mean, if he was, he'd be a super old cat by now."

"I don't know, Charlie. But I think anything is possible. Maybe cats come back. Or their spirits do. Maybe Benny is a relative of your Benjamin. I just know he adores you."

"Well, he's got a home with me for as long as he wants it. We'd better be quiet. They're stopped up ahead."

I hadn't even realized we'd made it back to the resort. Flashing red and blue lights lit up the parking lot, and there was a crowd of people outside, staring at us. I gripped Jasper tighter as he tensed in my arms.

"I'd better take him to my cabin, Charlie. I'll be right back."

She nodded and went to join Danny while I hurried towards my cabin. As I opened the door, I remembered what Ethan said. I usually locked my door and rarely forgot to. How had it been unlocked?

I turned on the light and saw Luna blinking at me sleepily.

"Oh, good, you're alright. Jasper was worried sick."

I closed the door behind me and walked over to the bed.

"How did you know I was in trouble, Jasper?"

He licked the fur I'd rumpled. His golden eyes gleamed as he looked at me.

"We're connected. You're mine and I'm yours. It runs deep within us. I'm just glad we got to you in time and that detective of yours showed up and let me out."

"Did you unlock the door?"

Jasper's eyes twinkled before he looked away.

"I don't have thumbs. How could I do something like that?"

He kept bathing, leaving me in the quiet with my thoughts punctuated by the soft meows coming from Luna's corner. I glanced at the mother cat, but she avoided my gaze. Something had happened, but I had no clue what it was.

"I'd better go back and talk to Ethan. I'll return as soon as I can and I'll make sure you both have some treats, okay?"

Jasper purred as I stroked his head before walking over to the door. I stared at the locking mechanism and looked back at the bed.

Had I forgotten to lock it? I finally shrugged, mystified. Maybe I'd never know how it happened.

I trudged back through the snow towards my friends and Detective Rhodes. Charlie wrapped an arm around me as Danny was looked over by the paramedics. They gave him the all clear, and he shuffled over to us, smiling.

"Guess I've got a hard head."

"Well, I for one am glad you do," Charlie said, shocking both of us as she leaned over and pressed a kiss to Danny's cheek. "You were a hero out there. You thought fast and kept them from finding that phone."

Danny blushed a fiery red.

"Nah, I'm just me. Hey, what happened to my road cobbler? I wasn't done with that."

Charlie rolled her eyes.

"Seriously? You're worried about your dessert?"

"That was a seriously good cobbler. And I'm hungry after all of that. I think I deserve a small bowl of cobbler after tonight."

He put on a pious expression that made Charlie laugh even harder. She threaded her arm through his and shook her head.

"I'll see what we can do. I'm sure the kitchen's got some leftovers. We'll even warm it up and find some ice cream."

They wandered towards the dining hall, wrapped up in each other, and my heart sang. Maybe Danny's dreams of a relationship with Charlie were about to come true. I couldn't be happier. I felt Ethan's hand on my arm and turned to look at him.

"I know you're tired, but we'll need statements. It can wait until morning if you'd like. Your cat is okay, right?"

"He's fine. Let's just get the statements done tonight. I'm sure Danny and Charlie will be back soon."

"Now that's an interesting couple. They seem right for each other, though."

I looked into his sky-blue eyes and wondered if we were right for each other, too. Ethan seemed to read my thoughts, and he cleared his throat before opening his mouth to continue, only to be interrupted as a uniformed officer approached. He held up a hand in my direction before walking away a short distance.

It looked like the beginning of a long night, but I was alive to experience it. I'd finally come clean to my best friend, and she didn't hate me. Maybe that meant that someday, I could tell Ethan, too. I smiled as I looked in his direction, feeling braver than I had in a long time. I wouldn't tell him tonight, but soon. Maybe.

Until then, I had some kittens to help raise, Jasper to spoil, Benny to help, and all of my friends, cat and human, to share my life with. Things were looking up, and I couldn't wait to see what the future held for all of us.

KEEP READING to see what Eden and the gang are getting up to next!

Don't Miss Pushing Up Daisies

At long last, Spring has arrived at the Valewood Resort, and Eden Brooks couldn't be happier. Wildflowers are blooming and business is booming. After a rough few months at the resort, finally, everything is going right.

Eden teams up with a local mountain guide to provide wildflower tours to guests of the resort. Just when things couldn't get any better... they gets worse.

One of her tour guests ends up dead, and unfortunately, way too many people have a motive, including the mountain guide she hired. Eden gets tangled up in a web of deception, full of false starts, lies, and misdirection.

Luckily, some of Eden's special friends are visiting, because she's going to need all the help she can get to catch this killer, before she ends up pushing up daisies, too.

Fans of the Razzy Cat Cozy Mysteries will love this crossover! Coming in early Fall of 2024!

Books By Courtney McFarlin

A Razzy Cat Cozy Mystery Series

The Body in the Park

The Trouble at City Hall

The Crime at the Lake

The Thief in the Night

The Mess at the Banquet

The Girl Who Disappeared

Tails by the Fireplace

The Love That Was Lost

The Problem at the Picnic

The Chaos at the Campground

The Crisis at the Wedding

The Murder on the Mountain

The Reunion on the Farm

The Mishap at the Meeting

The Bones on the Trail

A Soul Seeker Cozy Mystery

The Apparition in the Attic

The Banshee in the Bathroom

The Creature in the Cabin

The ABCs of Seeing Ghosts

The Demon in the Den

The Ether in the Entryway

The Fright in the Family Room

The Ghoul in the Garage

The Haunting in the Hallway

The Imp at the Ice Rink

The Jinn in the Joists

The Kelpie in the Kennel

The Lady in the Library - Fall 2024

The Clowder Cats Cozy Mystery Series

Resorting to Murder

A Slippery Slope

A Mountain of Mischief

Pushing Up Daisies - Fall 2024

Millie the Miracle Cat Cozy Mystery Series

A New Beginning

Stacked Against Us

A Siren's Song Paranormal Cozy Mystery Series

The Wrong Note

A Major Case

Escape from Reality Cozy Mystery Series

Escape from Danger

Escape from the Past

Escape from Hiding

A Note From Courtney

Thank you for taking the time to read this novel. If you enjoyed the book, please take a few minutes to leave a review. As an independent author, I appreciate the help!

If you'd like to be first in line to hear about new books as they are released, don't forget to sign up for my newsletter. Click here to sign up! https://bit.ly/2H8BSef

A Little About Me

Courtney McFarlin currently lives in the Black Hills of South Dakota with her fiancé and their two cats.

Find out more about her books at:
    www.booksbycourtney.com

Follow Courtney on Social Media:

https://twitter.com/booksbycourtney

https://www.instagram.com/courtneymcfarlin/

https://www.facebook.com/booksbycourtneym

Made in the USA
Monee, IL
14 November 2024